THE LADY AND HER QUILL

The Ladies of Sommer-by-the-Sea
Book 1

Ruth A. Casie

ARE YOU SIGNED UP FOR DRAGONBLADE'S BLOG?

You'll get the latest news and information on exclusive giveaways, exclusive excerpts, coming releases, sales, free books, cover reveals and more.

Check out our complete list of authors, too!

No spam, no junk. That's a promise!

Sign Up Here

www.dragonbladepublishing.com

Dearest Reader;

Thank you for your support of a small press. At Dragonblade Publishing, we strive to bring you the highest quality Historical Romance from some of the best authors in the business. Without your support, there is no 'us', so we sincerely hope you adore these stories and find some new favorite authors along the way.

Happy Reading!

CEO, Dragonblade Publishing

Additional Dragonblade books by Author Ruth A. Casie

The Ladies of Sommer-by-the-Sea Series
The Lady and Her Quill (Book 1)

Pirates of Britannia Series
Donald
Hugh
Graham
The Pirate's Jewel
The Pirate's Redemption

CHAPTER ONE

London
November 1814

LADY ALICIA HARTLEY clutched the heavy parcel under her arm and hurried along Fleet Street through the thick fog. She took scant notice of the people rushing past her or the church bells chiming noon. New ideas fluttered and flittered through her mind. Success had led to opportunities she never dreamt possible until now. Her lips pursed as she tried to suppress a satisfied smile.

Caution. The small inner voice broke through her dreaming and her brows knitted together. *Don't be reckless.*

Alicia rubbed the amber stone she wore around her neck. The pendant was a gift from her father.

Confidence is everything, though, was one of Mrs. Bainbridge's guiding principles.

It started with Miss Whitlock. Since Alicia was a little girl, Miss Greta Whitlock had been her governess. Alicia was fond of the tall, pleasant woman who at times was more like an older sister. Some of her best memories were sitting in the window seat in the attic room, staring at the sea and just talking about hopes, aspirations, dreams, and well, everything. Nothing was prohibited. If anything, the woman encouraged her to be an independent thinker and draw her own conclusions.

Alicia soon became proficient in drawing, needlecraft, music, and dance. While only a passing knowledge of French and Italian was expected, Alicia excelled past songs and snippets of poems and stories presented in the romantic languages. Her natural curiosity eventually drove her to acquire fluency in both, and proficiency in Greek and Latin.

Her schooling included the practical study of household management that went beyond managing the staff and counting the silver, but also included training in hiring, purchasing, and gardening.

Decorum ruled a lady's life from her core to her habits. Nothing less was tolerated. Everything she did was scrutinized and criticized, but Miss Whitlock had done her job well.

They spent hours in the attic at her desk and looked forward to those days her father was not home. He agreed she could use his library when it wasn't occupied. She sat at the large table, surrounded by books, and enjoyed their sweet, musky scent.

Of all the subjects, her true love was writing – taking the actions, colors, sounds, and emotions of imaginary people and places she conjured in her mind and translating them into words for others to read and enjoy.

She had all but driven Miss Whitlock dizzy with her thirst for knowledge and her quest to improve her writing.

By the time she was fifteen, she mastered all the acceptable subjects a young woman was expected to learn and others some people would think unnecessary, a waste of time, or worse, *scandalous*.

With her parents' agreement, her governess sometimes submitted her essays to the village paper, the *Sommer Sentinel*. Mr. Leon Hawkins, the elderly owner, enjoyed her short story about *Margaret's Miracle*, a long-held folk tale about the village mayor's daughter Margaret and a Scottish trader. It was a reflective essay that spoke about the tale and introduced ideas based on facts she researched.

Hawkins also printed her more creative pieces. One in particular, her story that featured an upper-class lady and her plight in London society, had been very well received.

"You make me proud," Miss Whitlock had said, standing next to her at the library table, her hands clasped in front of her.

Proud. Alicia glowed brighter than the light from the oil lamp at the compliment.

"Put your books away and bundle up. It's bitterly cold out, and we're going to the tearoom today."

It was an innocent excursion. One they had made many times before. One she thoroughly enjoyed. Or was it the biscuits that drew her there?

When they arrived at the tearoom, Miss Whitlock led the way to a table by the window, where they joined another woman.

"Honoria, I'd like to introduce you to Lady Alicia Hartley."

Miss Whitlock turned to her.

"Lady Alicia, this is my dear friend, Mrs. Honoria Bainbridge."

Everyone knew Mrs. Bainbridge – if not in person, then most definitely by reputation. She was the head of the Sommer-by-the-Sea Female Seminary, an elite school that every girl in the district, if not all of England, wanted to attend.

One didn't *apply* to the seminary. Admittance was only by Mrs. Bainbridge's personal invitation.

She and Miss Whitlock took their seats. Tea was already laid and waiting for them. At first, Alicia thought she would be a silent observer and given an opportunity to occasionally add her voice to the conversation.

Instead, she sat at the table as if she was a pane of glass, one both women saw right through. As tea progressed, she became anxious, and she had no idea why.

"Lady Alicia." Pulled from her star-gazing, she faced Mrs. Bainbridge. "Have you seen the London papers? Edmund Kean has signed a contract with Drury Lane. He is to play Shylock in

The Merchant of Venice. They are expecting a comedy," Mrs. Bainbridge said as she picked up her teacup. "What do you think of the play?"

It was a straightforward question.

One she was prepared for. She had studied Shakespeare and knew the play. "To me, the play is a drama, especially when Portia, disguised as a lawyer, begs Shylock to show mercy to Antonio. Her speech on the quality of mercy is dramatic and moving." Alicia took a breath and leaned forward, eager to go on. "The characters are sensitive and engaging. I don't see this play as a comedy. Although, I do think there are scenes where Shakespeare inserts comic elements to provide relief for the story's tension. But is the play a comedy? Not to me."

Mrs. Bainbridge smiled and gazed at her thoughtfully, then turned to Miss Whitlock.

"With the cold temperatures this last month, the Thames has frozen. There are plans for a frost fair between Blackfriars Bridge and London Bridge on the first of February." Mrs. Bainbridge set down her teacup and sighed. "I was a little girl when they had the last one."

Alicia really didn't want to talk about Shakespeare or the frost fair. She stared out the window at the cold gray sky and willed herself to stay in her seat.

"I read your story in the *Sommer Sentinel.*"

Alicia whipped her head around and again faced Mrs. Bainbridge.

"Your story, the experience of a young upper-class woman who must navigate London society for the first time and falls in love with a social superior, was very good. I thoroughly enjoyed the way you re-created the social world. Your characters are sensitive and engaging. I like the way you let your reader experience their distress and tenderness.

"The conflict is well-planned and given with enough context to maintain a good pace and keep your reader turning pages. You are a good storyteller."

Alicia felt her face flush at the compliment. "Thank you, Mrs. Bainbridge. I'm glad you enjoyed the story."

"I do see room for growth."

Alicia stared at the woman and tamped down her annoyance. What was wrong with her writing?

She didn't think the headmistress would wait long to tell her.

"Draw out the conversations. Just because *you* know where it is going does not mean your reader does. And give a little more exposition within the narrative itself as an anchor."

"It is very kind of you to give me some direction. I will certainly keep your comments in mind."

"I expect you will. I see a young person eager to succeed. You will, you know. You are a gifted storyteller."

Mrs. Bainbridge gave her a smile, not one of those smiles that didn't reach the eyes, but a smile that came from her heart.

Alicia took a biscuit and finished her tea. She gave Miss Whitlock a fleeting glance. Her governess sat proudly by as she engaged in a conversation with Mrs. Bainbridge.

She liked her governess, but she wanted to learn more. In truth, she longed to be under Mrs. Bainbridge's tutelage. The headmistress worked with her students to create a plan filled with courses that surpassed anything Miss Whitlock could teach. Some were usually only available to men.

Mrs. Bainbridge's words kept repeating in her head.

You are a gifted storyteller.

With tea over and the snow beginning to fall, they said their good-byes and departed.

"What do you think of Mrs. Bainbridge?" Miss Whitlock asked as they walked along the river.

"She's an excellent judge of writing talent."

Miss Whitlock stared at her for a heartbeat or two before she burst out laughing. "Yes, she is," she concluded. "And I think she gave you excellent advice."

Mr. Dodd, the butler, opened the door as they reached it.

Alicia and Miss Whitlock went into the drawing room, laughing like schoolgirls. The soft scent of violet on the air announced her mother was present.

"Did you have a nice outing?" Lady Hartley said, looking over her spectacles as she stitched a sampler.

"It was wonderful. We had tea with Mrs. Bainbridge. And I was careful, I didn't spill my cup and I only took one biscuit."

Lady Hartley smiled and put down her stitching. "Yes, I know you can be quite civil when you put your mind to it."

"Mrs. Bainbridge complimented me on my essay that was in the *Sentinel*."

"Then she must have good literary taste," her mother said. "Before I forget, you received a letter."

"It must be from Hattie in London. She told me she'd write to tell me when she was returning to Sommer-by-the-Sea." Alicia took the dispatch from the salver and opened the letter.

She took a seat next to her mother, read the contents, then stared at the note without saying a word.

"Alicia, is anything wrong? I've never seen you so quiet," her mother said, glancing at Miss Whitlock.

Alicia looked at her governess, then her mother.

"What is it?" her mother asked.

"It's an invitation." Her heart was beating so loud she was sure her mother could hear it. She lifted her chin. "Mrs. Bainbridge has invited me to be a student at the Sommer-by-the-Sea Female Seminary."

LOOKING BACK, SHE had no idea that tea with Mrs. Bainbridge would change her life. That was seven years ago. She spent five wonderful years at the Sommer Female Seminary learning everything she could. Now, two years later, she still heard Mrs. Bainbridge's words warning caution.

She clutched the parcel to her chest. This completed project was a good one. Better than her last. As soon as she presented it to Mr. Caulfield, he too would be enthusiastic.

Remain calm. Be gracious and pleasant but remain firm.

By the time she had mentally repeated the words several times, her doubts quieted. Of course, Caulfield would bargain. She would remind him their past achievements were for the most part her doing. She no longer wanted to sell her story to Caulfield Publishing for a fee and receive nothing beyond that. Her books sold well and made a profit, but only for Caulfield.

The sales gave her the confidence to ask for a change in their financial arrangement on this last book in her contract. She would gladly pay all the production costs for publication. Caulfield Publishing would distribute them and get ten percent from the profits, a reasonable and more equitable financial arrangement. It would also give her more control of her work. She pressed her parcel closer to her chest. If he wouldn't budge, there *was* the letter that arrived in yesterday's post.

How could he refuse?

Her smile dropped and her step faltered. Question her project, perhaps, but refuse? He couldn't. He wouldn't. Would he? A cold chill that had nothing to do with the weather ran up her spine.

A passing carriage startled her, shaking her out of her moment of distraction. Alicia looked about. Temple Church was to her right. Her destination wasn't much further. She resumed walking, but at a slower pace.

What if he did not agree to her request? She stared at the ground as if by some miracle the answer lay at her feet.

"I admire your conviction, Alicia, but you can't always have your way. In all things there is a give and take, a bargaining. Coming to a mutual understanding is the way both you and the other person will be successful."

More wisdom from Mrs. Bainbridge. The woman had an uncanny way of always seeing the truth of a matter.

It would be best for her to be prepared to listen, then bargain.

See a way for both she and Mr. Caulfield to come away a winner. Satisfied she had a plan, she quickened her step, eager to come to an agreement with her publisher and present him with her finished manuscript. She crossed Fetter Lane and came to her destination, Number 32.

Alicia entered the building, climbed the stairs, and stood at the door to Caulfield Publishing. Isaac Caulfield was a congenial gentleman for the most part, but occasionally he acted like most men—opinionated, closed-minded, and unrelenting.

Caulfield Publishing was not the first publisher she approached. She had set her sights on the renowned William Lane. With grace, he declined her manuscript and advised her the best and probably *only* way her story would be published was if she paid to have it printed and sold copies to her family and friends.

As an afterthought, he suggested a small, unknown company, Caufield Publishing.

She returned home heartbroken. Her sister, Beatrice, and brother-in-law, Captain Douglas Elkington, tried to soothe her. She told them Mr. Lane suggested another publisher, one more willing to produce her type of story. It was Elkington's approval that made her consider the idea. Intent and undeterred, she approached Isaac Caulfield.

He was not enthusiastic when she brought him her first manuscript.

Not at all.

He was ready to reject her story before he read a single word. Desperate, she cajoled him into reading the piece before he passed judgement.

That was two years ago. Now, their business arrangement was a successful one. Earlier this week Caulfield released and sent her fifth book, *The Lost Dowry*, to the library on Leadenhall Street.

Her triumphs were on her side.

Alicia took a deep breath, straightened her spine, turned the latch, and entered. "Good day, Mr. Caulfield."

The publisher sprang to his feet.

"Lady Alicia." He pulled out his pocket watch. "You're early. What a pleasant surprise. Please, be seated."

"I apologize for my early arrival, but I am eager to speak with you."

"Are you here alone?" He came to her side and glanced out the door.

"Yes." She winced at the trace of defiance in her voice. Another social blunder. Beatrice warned her *London* propriety was different from that at home in Sommer-by-the-Sea. It amazed her that a different world existed three hundred miles south of the village.

A chaperone.

The idea made her teeth itch. Today, Beatrice was otherwise engaged and in truth, Alicia's patience ran thin waiting for her.

She stepped inside. The office was cramped not because it was small, but because it was in disarray. Everywhere she looked, there were books and papers. Dark walnut bookcases stuffed with unorderly books lined the left side of the room. Light filtered through bedraggled curtains on the large windows to her right. Several stacks of papers filled Mr. Caulfield's desk, which was positioned in front of the window. Similar bookshelves were on either side of the fireplace on the far wall – but were hidden behind a pile of papers on a second desk across from Caulfield's. The clutter of papers and books rendered that desk unusable. A modest fire burned in the grate to take off the chill.

She was surprised the entire place didn't go up in flames.

She stepped with care around crates that littered the floor, removed the *London Gazette* laying on the chair, and settled into the seat.

"My sister was unavailable to join us. She and her husband are preparing the family for a trip north to join our parents for the village's Harvest Festival. I wanted to speak to you before we left."

Had he heard her? She followed his stare. He was focused on the *Gazette* in her hand. She glanced at his desk, the chair next to her, but there was no place to put it.

"I'm leaving with the family for Sommer-by-the-Sea. I look forward to reading at Mrs. Miller's Circulating Library. I wanted to thank you for seeing that my books were delivered."

"You're most welcome. I'm sure reading small segments of your story will encourage people to either borrow or buy your book. I am glad you're here. I wanted to speak to you today on another subject. I too, will be leaving London." He reached for the *Gazette*. "Here. Let me have the newspaper, if you please."

Alicia took a quick look at the headline: *Missing Walmer Castle Chest Found – Empty?*

She glanced at Caulfield's extended hand. She was about to give the newspaper to him when she spotted a corner of the paper was turned down, exposing the book review page. She opened the paper and stopped.

One review was circled: *The Lost Dowry*.

She read the article out loud.

"This is the fifth little story by Lady Alicia Hartley. While her other stories held promise, this book does not reach the standards the author established in her previous publications. Perhaps the author's muse has gone astray. The characters and conflicts in *The Lost Dowry* had potential but only the heroine, who is quite good, shines. It is unfortunate that the others appear to have lost their way. They are forced, mechanical, and obstruct the story. In a word, they are disappointing. In this story..."

Skipping the summary of the plot, she went to the final paragraph.

"She should read J. C. Melrose's *In My Brother's Shadow* or any of the other eight stories in that series. *There* is an author who evokes a man's emotion, albeit the author could use some assistance with the female point of view. Can you imagine if these authors combined their skills? They would lay out a plot with characters that would keep you reading until the last page or the last flicker of your candle."

The newspaper trembled in her hand. She went back to the beginning of the article to find the name of the reviewer. Anonymous.

The coward.

Her eyes focused on the review. The small quakes and quivers of the paper she held attested to the state of her nerves.

"How did an appraisal of my story turn into a review for…" Her words clipped, her tone chilly, she spoke with as reasonable a voice as she could manage and scanned the article. "J. C. Melrose?"

She lowered the paper. Mr. Caulfield's lips moved as the empty feeling in her stomach built into a furious storm. She wasn't aware of anything he said, until his words filtered through at last.

"Lady Hartley, are you listening? Reviews like this are…not unusual. Keep in mind, you can't please every reader. I'm glad to publish your little stories."

"*Little stories.*" Her heart galloped like a horse in the steeple chase. Her hand touched her pendant. *Remain calm.*

But soothing herself was getting more difficult by the moment. Even rubbing her stone didn't help now.

People were buying her novels, all of them. Alicia thrust the offensive paper at him.

"Perhaps we should give the readers some time. We plan to publish your next story in the summer. I want to speak to you about my plans for the company. I've bought a new press—"

"The plan was for my new story to be published in February. Now you want a delay? Or do you mean to cancel our agreement?"

His face closed, as if guarding a secret. Her heart sank. He accepted this review. He may be tolerating her tirade, but he agreed with Anonymous.

Unable to remain calm a moment longer, she shot him a penetrating glare as she rose, her parcel in hand.

"Not at all." He sprang to his feet, his chair scraping the floor behind him. "Being an author is not easy, Lady Alicia. I warned you before we began you would be at the mercy of the reading public, a capricious lot. I knew you were persistent and had promise." He studied her over the rim of his glasses. "I believe you still do, but with the new press I have plans to—"

But.

How often had she heard that insignificant word in front of every variation of the word *no*, a weapon men used to deny a woman her due?

"This is one review." Alicia paced the small space in front of his desk. "Caulfield Publishing has published five of my," she turned and faced him, "'little stories' to your financial advantage."

He gave her a sheepish glance.

"Before I let you read this..." She paused and held up her parcel. "I'll give your suggestion to delay publishing more thought, *then* send you my decision."

As disappointment and despair dimmed her enthusiasm, she questioned what happened to yesterday's excitement and celebration. *The Lost Dowry* was in the circulating library. Congratulatory notes from friends were piled on the salver on the foyer table.

And there was the letter.

She couldn't believe her good fortune when she read William Lane's message, although Elkington believed it. She had never seen her brother-in-law so excited. He took out the sherry and they all toasted the occasion. But now...her dream was dissolving in front of her eyes.

How could one awful review ruin everything? Mr. Lane would not want to read her manuscript now, and Mr. Caulfield questioned publishing her next story. Remaining calm was out of the question.

Her secret was out. She had done a good job and convinced

herself and everyone else Lady Alicia Hartley was an *author*.

Everyone but one reviewer. Her breath came in small bursts. She stared at the *Gazette* on his desk and wanted to tear it to pieces.

"Lady Alicia, please sit down. We'll discuss this and come to a decision that is satisfactory to us both."

She glanced at the man, remained motionless, and held her words behind her teeth, not trusting herself to speak. Afraid she'd say something she would regret, Alicia turned and marched to the door with as much dignity as possible.

"My 'little stories,' as you like to refer to them, are all the rage."

She grabbed the latch and hoped he didn't observe her trembling hand or her watery eyes. At the moment, her single thought was to escape.

"Please, come sit and we can discuss our course of action without any—"

"Womanly emotions?" Her voice was heavy with sarcasm.

"No, not at all. I've been trying to tell you about some changes."

"Another time, perhaps. My family is traveling north, and I mustn't delay." By all that was holy, she needed to get away from the man.

"I understand. My regards to your sister and brother-in-law." He called to her as she pulled open the door and collided into a solid obstacle. Startled and thrown off balance, Alicia lost her grip on her parcel and sent the bundle tumbling to the floor.

Strong hands grasped her shoulders to steady her. Alicia's head snapped up. She stared into concerned gray, silver-streaked eyes. She took a deep breath and was surprised by the scent of lavender and citrus.

"I... I... forgive me, sir." She lowered her gaze to the gloved hand on her right shoulder and back to his penetrating stare. "Release me, please. I assure you I have recovered."

The man's concerned expression vanished, replaced with a

humorous glint. He removed his hands and stepped away.

His great coat flowed around him as he bent and retrieved her parcel from the floor. Her shoulders felt the ghost of his strong yet gentle grasp. As he stood, she looked away eager to leave.

"There is nothing to forgive." He bent his head toward her and handed her the bundle. "I, too, would want to make a fast escape from Mr. Caulfield."

"Thank you," she said without any humor, pulling the parcel close.

"My pleasure, I assure you." The gentleman tipped the brim of his hat.

Alicia turned and rushed down the stairs.

JUSTIN CAULFIELD ENTERED his uncle's office. He glanced around, but found no place for his hat. He settled on putting it on the stack of books on the mantel.

"Lady Alicia is a determined woman." Isaac went to the grate for a taper to light his pipe. "And she was correct."

So, that was the illustrious Lady Alicia Hartley. Ever since his uncle shared the accounts with him, he'd been going on and on about the woman and her so-called little stories. That the man was distressed was an understatement. What had upset him and his treasured author?

"Correct? What do you mean?"

"She is correct that her stories generate a considerable amount of money for the company. I won't lose her. Her reaction to that review surprised me." His uncle pointed to the paper. "She's received other reviews that have not been favorable. But this one upset her."

Justin picked up the *London Gazette*.

"Don't blame yourself. She would have read or heard about

this in due course." He tossed the paper onto the desk without reading the review. "We both are aware reviews are subjective. An author will not please everyone. Did you get my message?" His uncle asked, then looked up at him.

"I found it when I arrived last night. I'm going to visit Lord Barrington in Sommer-by-the-Sea and will make your delivery for you. How did your favorite author react when you told her you were retiring to the country, and a new publisher and editor was taking your place?" Justin leaned over the desk and searched through the papers in the in-basket.

"I tried more than once to tell her my plan, but the woman didn't give me the opportunity."

Justin, still bent over the basket, stopped his search and glanced at his uncle.

"You didn't tell her."

"Her new manuscript was in that parcel. But she was like a dog with a bone and wouldn't let go of the review. I suggested we publish the story later in the year, perhaps this summer."

Justin straightened and put down the papers that were in his hand. "Let me guess. That's when she rose to her feet and stormed out."

"Near weeping. I prayed she would keep them at bay. I can't abide a woman's tears. I'm certain she doubts my confidence in her writing. But I assure you, I'm quite convinced of her ability. I wanted to inform her of our plans for the company. About you stepping in, but the *Gazette* review held her full attention." The man leaned forward with his face flushed in anger. "A dog with a bone, I tell you."

"Now, now. There is no need to get upset. She is emotional and will come around if she wants her next story published."

"My intent to delay publishing her story had nothing to do with that… that article." He pointed to the *Gazette*. "I wanted the new publisher, you, to work with her on her story."

"It's not easy listening to criticism of your work." He held papers in his hand and stared at the desk. A heartbeat later, he let out an exasperated sigh and returned to his search. "I know. I've had my share of disappointing reviews. Whether I work with her or not, I don't agree with you putting off her publication date. If anything, I would publish her next story ahead of schedule. Releasing a new book close to this review may be to your advantage. If the review is as bad as you say, a new release could encourage curiosity."

"That may not be a bad idea." His uncle sat back in his chair. The flush subsided from his face. "I leave the decision up to you and her."

"You're not out the door yet."

"No. I'll always be close. But dealing with creative people is not easy. Their work is an integral part of them, and at times they are not able to separate their story from themselves. Like the reviewer has his bias, the author has theirs. To them, their work is perfect. Take *your* writing."

"My writing? I thought you enjoyed my stories. I write big ones, not little ones." He teased his uncle. He was halfway through the pile.

"I do enjoy your stories. Big or little, they are excellent. Your understanding of soldiers and the battlefield are exceptional. It's no surprise to me that Lord Barrington and the Duke of Wellington call on you even though you are no longer in the service. You're the epitome of a fine Highland warrior."

Justin, with one eyebrow raised, gave him a sideways glance. "Me? A *fine Highland warrior*. You've been reading too much Walter Scott." He returned to looking through the papers.

"You mock me? Well, I'm not surprised. You always did underestimate your abilities. Put you in a kilt with a claymore in your hand, and your bloodline will show. It did on the battlefield. You were fierce – a force few men wanted to cross. But it is much more than your broad chest and handsome knees. There is another side to the Justin Caulfield I know."

"And what is that other side?" he asked, chuckling, still digging through the pile of papers.

"There is a very human side to you. I remember the rambunctious lad who filched tarts from the kitchen, ran the fields with his friends, and stood up to those who thought to bully him. You weren't fast to take to your fists, no. You tried to settle things with words. But when needed, you stood up for yourself and others. You never backed down. You've grown to understand what drives people. You don't abuse it, but rather, you help them to be their best. It is what makes you a good leader... and you bring all that knowledge and expertise to your stories. However, even they have room for improvement." His uncle glanced briefly at the door. "You could learn a few things from Lady Alicia. It says as much in the *London Gazette*."

Justin picked up the paper and searched for his book on the review page.

"Where? There is no review of my story here." He gave his uncle a questioning stare.

"Read the review for *The Lost Dowry*. The reviewer mentioned you as well." The publisher pointed to the paper in his hand. "The last paragraph."

The room was quiet except for the fire snapping in the grate. His uncle worked on the papers in front of him while Justin read the review.

"Anonymous likes my Captain Mallory well enough." Justin's mouth curved into an unconscious smile as he continued reading.

His amusement quickly died. He lowered his hand to his side still holding the *Gazette*.

"By all that is holy," he said, his Scottish brogue unmistakable in his words. "What does he mean, I need assistance with the *female* point of view?"

A mention in a review of her book? Not even a review of the entire story. He reeled as he re-read the paragraph and grasped the meaning. *Rubbish. Learn from Lady Alicia?* An absurd idea. He gave an indifferent chuckle, returned the paper to his uncle, and continued to search the basket while he seethed.

"You laugh. Read her stories. Especially her last—"

"The one with the scathing review?" Justin interrupted, not lifting his head.

"Read it, Justin, and you will understand my meaning. She portrays her female characters in a unique manner."

"How do you accept a review from someone who is ashamed to use his name, or…" Justin picked up his head and gave his uncle a questioning glance. "Do you know who wrote it?"

"I spoke with Herbert, the editor of the *Gazette*. Questioned him about the review. He confided one of their trusted reviewers wrote the piece."

"Could Anonymous be a competitive author?"

Would an author question a fellow writer's work publicly for their own gain? The idea was not impossible.

"No. Not at all. This was a constructive review." Uncle Isaac sat in his leather chair with an air of authority. His adamant response startled Justin.

The man protected the woman as if she were his own daughter. Justin had no intention of conducting business in such a manner when *he* took over the reins.

Where is that list? He didn't have time to spend all day here.

"*What* are you pecking around for?" His uncle pulled his chair closer to the desk.

"The titles of the books you wanted me to deliver to Mrs. Miller."

"I've sent the list to the press room and asked that the books be bundled and ready for you tomorrow. Pick them up on the press floor before you leave in the morning."

He put the papers in his hand back into the basket.

"I'm finished here. I'll see you when I return from Sommer-by-the-Sea." Justin stood and retrieved his hat from the mantel.

"You have my thanks."

"What are you thanking me for? Your request was not inconvenient. I already had plans to stay there." Justin glanced at him. The man was full of surprises today.

"Mrs. Miller has a solid business and increases her orders with us each month."

Justin inclined his head and murmured, "She's an important client and needs special care."

"True, but my gratitude extends beyond you delivering the books. Your idea to purchase a new iron press was brilliant. The men were spending more time repairing the old one than printing. The quality of the books, as well as the quantity, is much improved as well.

"I had no one to take over the company. That is, until you came to us. Your stories, your leadership, and your ideas proved to me you were the perfect person to succeed me. I decided then and there I would leave you with everything in place, the authors and updated equipment. I'm eager to see how you will grow the company."

Justin had suggested the purchase months ago. However, once his uncle approached him to be his successor, he was sure his plans had changed. Justin saw his responsibility as *winding down* Caulfield Publishing.

Buying a new press was not the action of a man closing his business.

No one was more surprised than he was when he met Lord Stanhope at White's. His lordship told him all about the hard bargain his uncle struck with him.

"And that's not all. Your Aunt Lavinia is making demands on my time, and I haven't yet retired. I've worked hard to make Caulfield Publishing a success. You are loyal and worthy to be my successor. I leave the business in your capable hands. Now, be off with you before I say something sentimental."

Justin hesitated a moment before he put on his hat, avoiding his uncle's stare, afraid the man would see his shameful expression.

"Have a safe trip," his uncle said. He picked up a manuscript from the stack on his desk and began to read.

He loved his uncle for his encouragement, support, and sincerity. He built a small but mighty company that was sound, from the work he produced to the income he made. This turn of events was unforeseen.

Loyal. Worthy. Capable hands.

Justin closed the door behind him. His blood turned cool as he went down the stairs. He left the building and at the corner, removed a letter from his pocket.

His uncle pushed him to be more ambitious with his writing.

"Seek out a publisher who can get you places I can't."

He could have strangled the man for sending Lane his manuscript without telling him.

The unsolicited message from William Lane Publishing informed him that he was one of two authors under consideration for the last position on their list. The message came at the right time, or so he thought. He had to find another publisher with Caulfield Publishing closing. This was the opportunity he and his uncle had spoken about months ago.

He glanced up at the office window. His uncle never planned to close the company. He walked on. What was he to do now?

CHAPTER TWO

THE BLUE MAIL coach with its red painted wheels stood outside the White Horse Tavern and Family Hotel on Fetter Lane not far from Fleet Street. The lead horse's hind quarter shivered in the cold breeze. People were bundled against the light wind that made its way up the lane from the river.

The door to the inn opened as one of the passengers, a vicar, came out carrying a small bundle wrapped in a serviette surrounded by the aroma of fresh bread and cooked bacon.

Justin approached the waiting mail coach. "I'll take that, sir." The driver reached for Justin's portmanteau to secure it to the top of the coach. "Would you like that parcel on top as well?"

He glanced at the overcast early morning sky. With the chance of rain, he didn't want to risk the books being damaged.

"No. I'll keep it with me."

He hoped they would depart before the skies opened. The last thing he wanted to do was sit for hours in damp clothes.

The driver fixed the last of the luggage to the top of the coach and came down to help the passengers settle into their seats. Four other passengers shared the coach with him. Luckily, the last passenger decided to ride with the driver. The coach would have been cramped, but they would have made do.

"We will be traveling through the night and stops will be as long as it takes to change the teams and drivers," the driver said, leaning into the cabin. "Be at the coach ready to leave or you will be left behind. I don't wait."

His short speech completed, he turned up the step and closed the door. The carriage rocked as he boarded and took his seat. With a gentle click of his tongue, the team started lurching the coach forward.

They made slow progress through the London streets. The clouds had grown more ominous and by the time they reached the edge of the city a light drizzle was falling.

Late autumn on England's east coast had been exceptionally dry this year, leaving the rutted dirt road hard-packed. The rain wouldn't soak into this soil. If it rained hard enough, water would fill the ruts and turn the ground to mud. The going would be bad for the horses and twice as difficult for the coach. There was no help for it.

"Good morning," he said to the vicar. "It looks like we are in for some rain."

"Good morning, sir. I'm afraid I agree with you. The weather doesn't appear promising for our journey. I am Lucas Sheridan, a vicar from Harrogate, and you, sir?"

"Mr. Sheridan." Justin nodded. "Captain Justin Caulfield."

"Let me introduce you to Mrs. Gibbs and her boy Jim." The vicar turned to the woman and boy. "Captain Justin Caulfield."

The woman smiled pleasantly. The boy, no more than six, yawned and cuddled next to her.

"Sit up and say hello," she said to her son. "Please forgive him, Captain."

"No need to apologize," he said.

"Good morning, sir." The boy turned back to his mother and played with his fingers. His mother repeatedly quieted his hands with a gentle pat. The poor fellow was tired, bored and likely not excited about the trip.

The vicar was pleasant and dutifully listened to Mrs. Gibbs as she went on and on and *on* without any indication of stopping. He did speak up every now and then, possibly just to hear another voice.

The other passenger, Mr. Pratt, had chosen to join the driver and sat outside. Justin couldn't blame him. It was one way to avoid the incessant chatter of Mrs. Gibbs. He would have joined him, but not in this weather.

He was comfortable considering the cramped quarters. He settled in his seat by the window where he could easily access the writing table and faced the back.

The high-backed benches were covered with tufted leather. The straw stuffing was worn, but adequate. The glass windows closed to the stench from the London streets were covered with cotton shades.

No air circulated inside the small space and while it was cold outside, it was close inside and he was sweating. He couldn't wait until they were outside the city, and he could open the window for a bit of fresh air.

As they crossed the River Lea on the outskirts of London, large drops of rain began to bombard the coach. So much for fresh air. It was going to be a long, uncomfortable ride.

By the mid-afternoon when the coachman stopped in Cambridge to change the team, the drizzle had become a steady downpour and the rain-filled ruts had turned the road to mud. Several times he, Mr. Pratt, and the vicar helped the driver free the wheels.

The first two-hundred miles were by far the worst. The constant cold rain made the journey difficult for the driver to maintain his schedule. The day-and-a-half trip would be a cold, wet three-day ordeal.

After two-and-a-half days, they reached Harrogate in West Yorkshire. He said adieu to the vicar, Mrs. Gibbs, and Jim. Mr. Pratt tipped his hat, waved, and was gone before Justin retrieved his portmanteau and brought it into the cabin with him.

The road on the other side of Harrogate appeared to be in better condition. The rain hadn't been as damaging here. With any luck, the coachman would make up some time. He continued alone for the remaining eighty-five miles to Newcastle, then an additional five miles north to Sommer-by-the-Sea.

Without his fellow travelers to distract him, he removed a pencil and paper from his luggage and pulled open the small desk to begin planning his next book. He sat for some time, but the rhythmic beat of the horses' hooves and the rocking cabin along with two nights of inadequate sleep lulled him into a stupor.

Unable to concentrate on a story, he pushed the curtain aside, opened the window a bit, and took a deep breath.

After days of rain, the blue sky with white clouds was a welcome change. He smiled reminiscing on the days he spent sitting on the slope of the hill by his home in Scotland. His face would be bathed by the sun as he stared at the clouds and he'd imagine the shapes they created: dragons, castles, ships.

Skies like this were made for cloud gazing. He let his mind wander. Today, there were no dragons. The clouds formed three straight lines, like soldiers called to order. A chilled rush of foreboding had his heart racing as ghostly faces materialized.

He turned away and scrubbed his mind. Mrs. Gibbs' droning voice would be a welcome distraction.

His head rested against the bench's high back as the vision faded. He let out a deep breath and scanned the coach, as if he wasn't familiar with every inch of it and was drawn to the bundle he'd taken from the press floor.

Eager for something to pass the time, he retrieved the parcel and pulled out a book. *The Lost Dowry*. He checked the others. It was filled with Lady Alicia's books. Not one copy of his.

A note addressed to him slipped out from between the books.

"Mrs. Miller is expecting you. Since I will not be attending her Harvest Salon, she has extended the invitation to you. I've told her she can depend on you for all things. Be prepared to read from your story."

A bit irritated with his uncle's directness, he let it pass. He represented his uncle at other events and this one was no different. Justin tapped the scrap of paper against his lips and stared out the window. Mrs. Miller was an important client. He would indeed attend her salon.

He tucked the message into his pocket and thumbed through a few pages not reading a word. Learn from Lady Alicia. What was she capable of teaching him? *Swooning, fashion, seduction, and whatever other frivolity she writes about.* He tossed the book across to the empty seat. It landed in his open luggage.

He closed his eyes, but his mind wouldn't quiet. His uncle's voice echoed in his head. *Loyal. Worthy. Capable Hands.*

It would serve the man right after all his conniving for him to respond to Lane's letter. He closed his eyes. The fight drained out of him. At the heart of it, his uncle was a good businessman. Surely, he would understand the opportunity that Lane presented to him. He let out a slow steady breath and wiped his hands down his breeches. How had this situation happened? Succeeding his uncle was an honor and all he thought about since last New Year's when they discussed it.

It was his aunt and uncle who helped him through those early days when he returned from the war. He blotted out his broken engagement and his years of service. Told no one of his time with the Cameron Highlanders.

At first, they indulged him. One evening, his aunt spoke to him.

"You're a shadow of yourself. There are barely glimpses of the boy I know and love. Just when we see that man emerge you travel to the next family of a lost soldier, but when you come back to us and are just settling in, you're as somber as before. You've seen and done things that I can't imagine, but you can't hold it all in. You must let it go."

"What I've experienced is not for anyone's ears." That had already cost him greatly. *"The person who would understand, the only person I can confide in, is someone who lived through the battles as I did."*

"I understand." Her hand had tenderly covered his. *"This is for you."*

His aunt handed him a journal, quill, and ink. "If you aren't able to tell me, write it down. Burn the pages afterwards if you like. But you must let it go."

For days, he looked at the journal, perhaps it was weeks before he began to write, but once he started, he had no way to stop. He didn't want to. Sitting at his uncle's desk in the library he created Jonathan Calum Mallory of the Cameron Highlanders, Captain in the Royal Highland Regiment, a proud soldier loyal to his country, his men and his family.

The more he wrote about Captain Mallory, the more he came back to the living.

"Justin, your papers were on my desk; I thought they were one of the books submitted to me to review for publication. It wasn't until I finished reading that I realized it was your writing. This is exceptional." His uncle raised the papers in his hand. "This should be published. Your voice deserves to be heard. This story, your story, needs to be told."

Who would want to read a story about a soldier and what he faced in France and Spain? Aunt Lavinia looked on with a hopeful expression. He agreed to let his uncle publish the work for no other reason than to please his aunt. To his surprise, the book sold well.

Letters addressed to him began to arrive at the office. He received messages from soldiers who faced similar horrors and questioned what it was all for. These men spoke of their fears, their losses, and some even of their hopes. He had no difficulty reading the unspoken words, the emotion behind each soldier's struggles and cheered for them when they mentioned their personal victories.

These letters and the men that wrote them held so much meaning for him. He was thankful for each one.

The coach bumped along. With the sun shining through the window, he felt at peace, closed his eyes, and didn't open them until the coach came to a stop some time later.

The fragrance of the briny sea filled the air along with the sound of waves crashing in the distance and seagulls calling overhead.

He stuck his head out the window. They were stopped along a desolate stretch of road. The driver was hunched over attending one of the horse's hooves.

"We'll be underway as soon as I take care of Bessy here, sir. You have time to stretch your legs if you like."

Justin stepped out of the coach. The cold wind tugged at his great coat and ruffled his hair. He stood next to the coach and took in the view. They road wound endlessly in both directions along a barren rise. Drawn by the thunder of the waves, he walked through the tall grass toward the edge of the cliff. As he got closer, the building swells came into view and finally the waves crashing on the rocky beach.

Lost in the rhythm of the waves, he was caught up by the beauty of the sea. The stinging breeze invigorated him. The last time he came to Sommer-by-the-Sea he traveled by schooner. Over land gave him a very different perspective.

Now he understood why his commander Lord Reese Barrington preferred living here to London. Barrington spoke fondly of this calm and tranquil place. It was a stark contrast to the battlefields on the Continent and the ballrooms in London.

After mustering out of the service, he and Barrington stayed close, as did several other officers that had reported to him. They helped each other through rehabilitation and back to civilization.

Barrington left London for his family's country estate in Sommer-by-the-Sea, while Justin traveled through England and Scotland visiting the families of the men who served under him and didn't return.

Each one was another page that had to be written. Another man he refused to forget.

The past summer was the last time he was with Barrington. He stopped to visit his friend on his way to Edinburgh to pay his respects to another family of a fallen soldier.

Today's trip was different. The message from Barrington was a call to action for help with a delicate issue. Justin's cousin on his mother's side, Alasdair Lawson, requested he come to Edinburgh.

That had made him laugh. Barrington had no idea why Lawson wouldn't speak to him.

"Sir?" the coach driver called interrupting his thought.

The emergency over, the man was in his seat ready to go. Justin returned to the coach.

It would be good to spend time with Lawson. His stories were legendary. Many a time they were up late drinking ale, his cousin telling him about the old days as a reiver and free trader. Justin made sure to go to Scotland several times a year. It was time for some hearty ale and good company.

The coach entered Baycliff Woods. He pulled his watch from his pocket. They would be in Sommer-by-the-Sea in twenty minutes. He had plenty of time to deliver the books to Mrs. Miller and arrive at Barrington's at a decent time.

He tucked away the timepiece and enjoyed the forest. The tree canopy gave them little shade. The leaves that remained fell in a shower of color. The rich smell of the damp soil and decaying leaves were mixed with the tinge of salt air.

The muffled sound of the horses' hooves along with the clink of the metal fittings on their tack lulled him into a daze. It wasn't until they came out of the woods and had a clear view of the castle in the distance that he became wide awake.

The coach made its way down King's Way, through Westmore Commons to South Lane, and arrived at the Sommer Inn. Justin gathered his things and stepped out of the coach.

"I thought the coach would never arrive."

Justin swung around at the familiar voice.

"This is an unexpected reception," he said to Lord Barrington.

"I was leaving an appointment when your coach pulled up. Simon, Peter, and Nicolas arrived earlier this week. James will be here later. I'm glad you're here." Barrington threw his arm around his shoulders. "I could have used you at my appointment. Come with me. The others are waiting."

"You go on ahead. I'll meet you. I want to deliver this parcel to the Millers' circulating library. I won't be long."

"The library is on my way. Get in. You can leave your portmanteau with me. I'll have Giles settle you in. We'll talk on the ride."

They settled in the carriage. Before they pulled away, Barrington handed him the *Sommer Sentinel*, the village newspaper. "You were always my best information gatherer. I've been asked to assist with this," Barrington said, as he nodded toward the paper.

"*Missing Walmer Castle Chest Found – Empty?*"

"This was in the *London Gazette*. Why speak to you? Isn't this more your brother Edward's concern? I thought he was in the House of Lords."

Justin put the paper down beside them.

"Edward and I spoke about the issue. I gave him a suggestion."

"Now I understand." Justin relaxed and shook his head. "You made a suggestion and now are charged with delivering it. You taught me a long time ago to never offer suggestions."

"Who gave me the idea for The League? Oh, yes. Captain Caulfield." Barrington leaned close. "It is one of your better ones."

They both laughed.

"And here I thought we were just a group of retired soldiers who watched and critiqued the politicians and military," Justin said.

"I like to call it strategizing military solutions," Barrington said. "And don't tell me you don't enjoy the work. I see how you and the others come alive with a new challenge. I'm attached to this village. If they have a need, I see it as my civic duty to help them. In truth, I'd never ask any of you to do anything you weren't comfortable with."

"We all know that. And you're right. We too see it as our civic duty. Without any military support within a hundred miles, I can understand why the village would call upon its residents for help, especially those with military experience. I admit, I believe in The League and protecting and upholding the rights of others, but working for the House of Lords?"

"Read the article. The chest contained a king's ransom in gold."

Justin took the paper back from Barrington. "It says here the chest was found empty. Gold, free traders, smugglers, French brandy." Justin looked at his friend.

"Rumors from the sensible to the ridiculous are circulating everywhere. Those—" he nodded toward the paper, "Are the sensible rumors. Since the editor's son took over the *Sommer Sentinel*, the editorial comments are sensational in nature rather than based on facts and evidence. On another note, your visit to Lawson. His message wasn't very clear."

"I'm not surprised."

"He said it was an urgent matter," Barrington said, glancing at the paper.

"This?" Justin asked. "Lawson told me he retired. At least that was what we celebrated."

"That is what I've been led to believe. If the issue was about free traders alone, I would be enjoying the harvest festival and not involved in my brother's problem. However, one piece of information is too troubling to be ignored. The free traders frequent the Cinque Port."

"In Kent, where Walmer Castle is located." Justin was on full alert.

"Lawson reached out to me after he was contacted by a French nationalist. Your cousin runs with a questionable lot. Even he is not sure who is friend or foe. He must proceed with caution. He's on his way to Edinburgh and will arrive by Saturday."

"I understand your concern. I visit him often enough that no one will suspect my appearance. And here I thought he missed me."

"I'm sure he does. This mess needs to be sorted out and we have little time. We have to confirm what is happening and send our report to Edward and the Land Guard at Bamburgh Castle a week from Monday."

"Leave me here," Justin said as they entered the commons.

"The library is across the square."

Barrington reined in the horse.

Justin stepped out of the carriage and turned toward the building.

"Justin."

He stopped and glanced over his shoulder.

"I'm glad you're here." Barrington flicked the reins and pulled away.

Justin, with the parcel tucked under his arm, stood watching the carriage move on. "So am I," he whispered.

People walked gingerly around icy patches as fast as they could, eager to reach a warm destination. The masts of the ships docked in the harbor poked into the sky over the roof tops of the buildings in the square. He pulled his coat collar around his ears against the cold gusts and crossed to his destination.

The library was in a large building. Two large plate-glass windows with muntins dividing the sash into square panes were on either side of the entrance. Justin opened the door, setting off the small silver bell attached to its top. The tinkling announced to everyone that someone had entered.

Welcomed by a warm wave of heat, he turned down his collar and rubbed his hands together as he looked around. The establishment was a modest size. Every wall was fitted with shelves filled with books. Two long desks flanked the room where patrons picked up and brought back their selections. Several large tables were scattered around the room displaying books.

Mrs. Miller's establishment was no different than the circulating library on Leadenhall Street in London. Fashionable ladies sat in chairs scattered throughout the room. Even in this remote village, the ladies were here to see and be seen. Now he understood why his uncle wanted him to read his story here.

Eager to deliver his parcel and be on his way to Barrington, he headed for the gentleman behind the desk.

"Good day. I'm here to speak with Mrs. Miller."

"She is not available at the moment. Perhaps I can help you. I'm her husband, Charles Miller."

"I have brought books your wife ordered from Caulfield Publishing." Justin said and put the books on the desk.

"Yes, for the reading." Mr. Miller removed the books from their packaging. "People have been asking about the reading all week. We're anticipating a large group. Both authors that are reading have a large following."

"Both authors?" Justin paused.

"Yes, Lady Alicia and Mr. Melrose will each be reading excerpts from their new stories. Both are excellent writers."

Another of his uncle's surprises. He really had to talk to the man.

"Have you read both books?" he asked Mr. Miller. Possible characterization issues aside, what on earth would make anyone in their right mind put his military story with a romance?

"I just finished reading Mr. Melrose's story. I'm sure a gentleman such as yourself would enjoy his book. I've read several similar stories written by soldiers concerning their military service. Mr. Melrose gives a poignant, accurate accounting of war, and the issues soldiers face during and after battle."

Justin recognized the brief faraway expression in the man's eyes. He had seen it many times before.

"Where did you serve?" he asked.

Mr. Miller gave him that special smile that transpired between comrades-in-arms. They had an immediate understanding as if some secret word had been spoken.

"Sergeant Charles Miller, sir. I was in the East Devon Regiment at Vitoria."

Justin didn't miss the pride in the man's voice. The story of that regiment was well known. He knew what Charles had endured in Spain.

"Ah, with Wellington. Your infantry regiment formed part of the backbone of the duke's forces."

"And you, sir. Where did you command?"

Justin raised his eyebrow. The former sergeant chuckled. Justin smiled and relaxed.

"Captain Justin Caulfield of Cameron's Highlanders. My last battle was at Salamanca. It appears we both served under the duke in Spain."

"Justin Caulfield Melrose?" Miller plucked a copy of *In My Brother's Shadow* from the shelf behind him, turned, and stared at him. "J. C. Melrose?"

"At your service," he said with a gracious nod.

Mr. Miller stood and gazed at him, awestruck. You would think that Wellington himself entered the reading room. "My cousin mentioned your name, sir."

"Where did he serve?" Perhaps he would stop and speak to him if he had time.

"He didn't serve. Her husband, Richard Lewis, did."

"Richard served with me." Justin's smile faded and his voice lowered. "Mrs. Lewis. In Edinburgh. Jenny. She had received a letter about her husband's death. I went to pay her my respects."

Another chapter in his book of painful memories. Of course, he remembered Mrs. Lewis. He remembered them all.

"You visited her and her son last year. Eli is a fine boy," Mr. Miller said, a sadness in his voice. "He enjoys reading adventure stories. I gave the boy one of your books."

"I visited them in the summer. The lad was curled up in a chair in the garden reading. I smiled when I saw he had my book. It warms an author's heart when he sees someone reading, and enjoying, his story."

"You spent the afternoon with him telling him about his father and all he had done. I'm glad you spoke to him."

"Eli should be proud of his father." Justin took a deep breath before he went on. If only they knew the visit helped him as much as it helped the boy.

"He wasn't with his mother when I first spoke to her. She asked some painful questions. Richard's bayonet wounds were severe. Richard and I had seen too much. We were both aware he was dying."

The battlefield rose out of his memory to swallow him whole. The booming noise of the guns and cannons had quieted. A calm twisted his insides tighter and tighter and tighter. Worse sounds were to come. They came despite the time and distance that separated him from the battle. He would never escape the wind that blew across the field, carrying the moans and cries of the wounded and dying. Never escape the knowledge that his enemy, the Frenchman, would likely never pay for his crimes.

"Richard's last words were to his wife and son. Sacred words that I vowed to deliver for him. I honored that promise." Justin was quiet for a few minutes dragging himself back to the present. "Before I left, Eli told me he imagined Captain Mallory would be like me. I thought that was curious. That's when I gave him my calling card with my pen name. You think I had given him a gold coin. I remember Eli's questions and enthusiasm."

"Jenny and the boy often speak about that day. She was with-ering away to nothing before you arrived. She was a different woman after spending time with you. Knowing Richard didn't die alone was a relief for her. For us all. You have our entire family's gratitude."

"I'm glad I gave her, Eli, and your family some peace."

He graciously accepted Charles' gratitude. He took on this rite for the men and for himself. These visits, as difficult as they were, brought closure to those he visited as well as brought him peace. He should be thanking them.

"I've read your new story. You capture the action and sur-roundings accurately. Your attention to military detail is superb. I've used your story with my students."

"I'm flattered. I can't imagine how you would use my stories with students unless the subject is military tactics."

"Not at all. I teach art and literature at the Barrow School for Young Men in Newcastle. I read excerpts from your stories and ask my art students to draw them. Some of their renderings are impressive and it is not from copying another picture but translating your words into pictures. Your vivid descriptions make it possible. Afterwards, we discuss the story."

"You have my thanks for the review." Justin hesitated, contemplating if he should pursue the question on his mind. Could his writing endure a literary critic? His curiosity won out.

"Did you find the characters in the story convincing?"

"Your insight of the military character and what he goes through is wonderful. The mysterious villain that appears to thwart Mallory in every story is well done. I keep reading waiting for you to unveil him. I'm curious though. You describe Mallory agonizing over leaving his family. Yet, you have him and his wife simply say good-bye. Such a devoted wife, even an English one, would not merely wave him off to war no matter how much she believed he was doing what was right. I would expect that from someone who has difficulty revealing their sentiments.

"You didn't appear to have any difficulty feeling emotions earlier. They were clear to me when you spoke about Jenny and more so about Eli. Digging deeper into the emotions of the supporting characters in your story would change your *good* stories into great ones. Right now, the accurate explicit military details and action are what carry the story."

Emotion wasn't something an officer cultivated. The irony of what Miller said was the same counseling he gave to the families of the fallen men he visited. Could he do it *himself* was a different matter. He was afraid he had too much pent up inside to let out.

The one time he did confide in someone, the person on the receiving side...

No need to revisit that chapter of his life. Her words echoed in his head as he took a deep breath and sent the memory back to the darkness.

She didn't want to hear about his war, nor understand what tormented him. Forget it. Leave it behind. Pretend it never happened. That was when he left Scotland and went to London to stay with Isaac and Lavinia. He told them it was to be closer to Barrington. It was to get further away from *her* and her new husband.

"If you don't want to bring out the emotion in order to keep the military focus of this story, I would eliminate the details about your character's family and his emotional dilemma. Although if you ask me, the emotional side of the man will make for a well-rounded character."

"You've made some good points that I will take to heart. I won't take up any more of your time." Justin picked up Lady Alicia's books. "I'll put these on the table by the door for you."

Miller nodded his thanks.

Had he focused his attention on Mallory to the detriment of every other character? Justin headed for the door, his mind on his story.

CHAPTER THREE

THE CREW OF the *Sommer Wind* sailed the schooner through the ancient Sea Gate at the entrance to Sommer Harbor and eased the ship into its berth. Alicia, thankful the short voyage from London to Sommer-by-the-Sea was uneventful, was anxious to go ashore.

When she was ready to leave London, the weather had turned in the north and coaches were delayed. By the time she reached the White Horse Tavern and Family Hotel the mail coach had left. She dreaded the trip on the schooner. While she enjoyed the wind in her face, her stomach rebelled. At least on this trip she was too busy being upset with Anonymous to be aware of anything else.

From her vantage point at the rail, the dock was coated with frost that rimed every surface. Swirls of snow blanketed the ground, muffling sounds. Chimneys belched smoke into the air, promising warm dry hearths inside.

She made her way down the gangplank with the help of one of the crew and hurried across Water Street, up North Lane toward Oak Lane, to the shelter of the shops and homes.

Ice and the strong gusts made walking a challenge for every-one except the children who gladly slid over the ice, laughing as they went by. Some brave souls dared the weather. They hailed each other, not stopping, and moved on to their destination.

The wind tugged at her bonnet. Luckily, she had the foresight to secure the ribbon tightly under her chin. Alicia pulled her brown wool pelisse close and struggled navigating the deepening snow and ice-covered puddles with her portmanteau.

Her destination, the Sommer-by-the-Sea Female Seminary, was up ahead. It was in a fine townhouse on the north side of the village where several landed gentry and professional families resided.

Once inside, Alicia headed for the drawing room, which Mrs. Bainbridge opened every afternoon for her graduates. The room was elegant with hand-painted Chinoiserie pale green wallpaper, a screen with a similar motif, and blue and green fabrics that complimented the mahogany furniture. The center-point of the room was the white marble fireplace that was inlaid with green marble fluting. The glamorous additions to a classical style were a decorating masterpiece, and the envy of several mothers of Mrs. Bainbridge's students.

"You're all brave souls," she heard Mrs. Bainbridge say, as she stood outside the room and put down her portmanteau.

"Will Alicia be here? Father mentioned that the road from London was particularly dangerous and not many carriages managed to get through. The London mail coach was almost two days late."

"I was so looking forward to seeing Alicia. I'm glad you coaxed her to read her book at the circulation library. I wouldn't miss her reading for anything."

Alicia opened the door.

"I wouldn't miss it either, Pat. Your father was correct about the weather and coaches."

The women turned in unison. Alicia stood in the drawing room doorway with her hat askew. Mrs. Bainbridge sat on the divan holding the tea pot, about to pour. Patrice Edgemont – Pat, never Patty – was by the fireplace. Marianna Ravencroft, Anna and Harriet Manning, Hattie, sat in the chairs adjacent to the divan. She caught Euphemia Brandt, Effie, sitting across from

Mrs. Bainbridge reaching for a confection.

"Alicia, are you well?" Mrs. Bainbridge stood and hurried to her side. She helped Alicia off with her bonnet and placed it on the chair with her pelisse.

"The wind almost blew me away. I couldn't get away from the dock fast enough." Alicia headed toward the hearth and held her hands in front of the grate, eager to warm them.

"The dock?" Mrs. Bainbridge asked.

"I arrived on the schooner and came straight here." Alicia said as she rubbed her hands.

"By ship? I thought she disliked…"

Pat hushed Anna.

"Tea? Alicia. Or would you prefer some whiskey?" Mrs. Bainbridge, who had returned to her seat, had her hand poised over the tea pot.

The room was quiet.

Alicia looked at the women. They had been close ever since they were Mrs. Bainbridge's charges and remained that way long after graduating. This was the one place they were themselves without reproach or censure.

"Tea, if I may. Ladies, nothing pleases me more than your concern and friendship. My sister and her husband had to leave without me. I had work to do in London. When I was ready to leave, the weather stopped the passenger coaches, and I missed the mail coach. That is the reason for my unplanned sea voyage." With her hands now warm, well, at least she was able to flex her fingers, she turned and faced them.

"That is all very distressing," Anna said.

"I would be happy if that were all, but it's obvious I also have an enemy." She took the cup of tea from Mrs. Bainbridge and sat next to Pat, who ate a small cake with butter icing.

"Enemy. What happened?" Her friends stopped with whatever they were fussing and were abuzz with questions.

Alicia removed a scrap of paper from her reticule and handed it to Anna. "Read it if you like. The last paragraph is most insulting."

Anna read the article aloud. Alicia stared at nothing in particular. The words didn't sound any better when someone else read them.

"This last paragraph isn't terrible." Anna handed the paper to Effie, who wiped cake crumbs off her fingers on the linen before she took the scrap.

"Anonymous ended my review talking about another author." Alicia swirled her spoon in her teacup, tapping the sides in a frantic rhythmic beat.

"Be careful, dear. You'll crack the china," Mrs. Bainbridge said.

Alicia stopped mid-stir. Removed the spoon. Put it to the side.

"You don't take constructive criticism well," Pat said, picking crumbs off her plate and eating them. "That's all this is. Your heroine was brave and her hero daring. The story was deeply romantic."

"Pat." Effie covered her friend's hand with her own. "Ever since you met George, everything is *romantic*."

Pat smiled as Effie took another bit of cake. "Everything George *does* is…romantic."

Alicia coughed, choking on her tea.

"Oh, my. Are you all right?" Pat asked, pounding Alicia on her back.

"You're so wicked, Pat," Anna said.

"Just taking a lesson from Alicia's heroine." The devilish glow in Pat's eyes could not be missed. "I thought that dialogue was good when I read it. Is it plagiarism if you quote dialogue from a story?"

Alicia shook her head, a large smile on her face.

"Do you have any idea who wrote the review?" Mrs. Bainbridge asked.

"Not at all." Alicia took another sip of tea. Her insides were warming.

"Is the reviewer possibly another author?" Hattie asked.

"I haven't given it much thought." Alicia stared at Hattie over her teacup.

Hattie took the article. She opened a wooden box that hung on the wall exposing a dart board and pinned the newspaper in the center. She removed three darts from their case.

"Your turn." Hattie offered her the white darts, Alicia's favorites. "I made sure the word 'Anonymous' is in the center."

Alicia put down her cup and took the darts, stood a good distance from the board and aimed. The dart board was a relic from the previous owner of the house. Mrs. Bainbridge encouraged her girls to take aim at their problems, literally and figuratively. If questioned about the dart board's use, the appropriate response was the girls were building their hand-eye coordination.

Of course, she'd given thought to Anonymous' identity. She'd been thinking about who the critic was ever since she read the review.

She let loose her first dart. It hit the capital A in anonymous.

Excited to hand in her new manuscript to Caulfield, she hardly tasted her breakfast. There was enough time for her to deliver her story and be back in time to leave with her sister and family for the journey here. Everything was going well until she stepped inside Caulfield Publishing.

As soon as she walked into his office, she knew something was wrong. The man was not neat, but the disarray was beyond the pale. She noticed the review when she handed him the paper.

She took aim and let the second dart fly. This one landed on the next letter, n.

"Reviews like this are...not unusual. I've happily published your little stories. Keep in mind, you can't please every reader."

He wants to put off publishing her next book until the summer. Based on one review. *One* review. How could he?

She didn't take time to aim the last dart. As fast as she lifted it, she let it loose. It nested with her other two. Alicia removed the darts, returned them to their case and closed the board, but not before she removed the article. Alicia handed the scrap of paper to Hattie.

"No, you keep it." Hattie waved her away. "Put holes in his review just as you did in the paper it is printed on."

She returned to her seat and took another sip of tea, feeling much better.

"Thank you, Hattie. I feel like myself again."

Mr. Caulfield wasn't at all pleased when she told him she had yet to decide if she was going to submit her next book to him. She should have told him then and there about the letter from William Lane.

She stayed in London for two days after Beatrice and Elkington left, going through every word of *The Lost Dowry*, trying to make sense of the reviewer's comments. Her heroine didn't have to be the only one to succeed. The hero could have been more… heroic. She stared off into the room.

What made her expect to succeed? Anonymous certainly didn't think she should.

"Alicia, are you listening to me?" Effie asked.

"Obviously not. She's off in her world planning another great adventure," Anna said.

Alicia put her cup on the small table next to the chair.

"Of course. I'm listening."

"Have you read any of J. C. Melrose's stories?"

The mere mention of the author's name made her blood boil. To think her closest friend would suggest such a thing. Alicia got to her feet so fast she nearly knocked Effie over.

"Traitor."

Effie grabbed her arm before Alicia walked away.

"No. Listen to me. You remember when Mr. Lindsay was teaching us about the Romans and why they were so successful?" Effie said with quiet yet determined firmness.

Alicia stopped, a bit confused.

"Romans? What are you after? I could not care less about the Romans at the moment."

Alicia stared at her friend, waiting for her to finish her thought. How was this line of thinking relevant?

"Know your enemy," Anna said from across the room.

"Precisely." Effie's face filled with triumph. "Why did this reviewer who was too much of a coward to take credit for his work, make the comment? The way you find out is by reading J. C. Melrose's story."

Effie's idea *was* worthy. Alicia lowered herself back into her chair. More than worthy.

Effie shooed Pat away, sat in her seat, then took Alicia's hands.

"I love your writing and your characters. They are all rich with emotion. You create worlds in which I want to live and for a few hours I do. I want to be like your heroine, but her hero..." Effie stopped.

"No, please. Continue. I'm listening." Alicia sucked in a deep breath and braced herself. Effie had a way of being brutally honest.

"Your hero is not worthy of a woman like your Clarissa. I believe that is what Anonymous was saying. I'm angry after reading that review, but curious as well. What type of story did J. C. Melrose write that Captain Mallory is a man worthy of your woman? Read the story and come to your own conclusion. You may find that Captain Mallory is the man you've been looking for."

Alicia burst into laughter while she fiddled with her pendant. The double-meaning was not lost on her.

"What makes you say I'm looking for a man? Is that what you have in your mind that my writing is about? Well, not at all." Alicia turned to her hostess. "Thank you for the tea."

Effie of all people should appreciate why she wrote. She and Effie helplessly watched as Patrice's brother went on into an active, rich life while their friend, far more intelligent than her sibling, was relegated to managing the house and a loveless marriage. It wasn't just Patrice, it was what society expected, no, *demanded* from all of them. She had no desire to marry and be ruled by a husband.

No, her heroines did things they wanted to do without society's rules, boundaries, or judgements. She rose from her chair and smoothed her skirt.

"Ladies, if you will excuse me. I must go to the circulation library and make the final arrangements."

"Wait," Hattie said. "I'll go with you."

"No need for you to go out in this cold weather."

"I'll see you out," Mrs. Bainbridge said as she led her out of the room and closed the door.

"You've kept me on tenterhooks long enough. In your last letter you said you had exciting news. Aren't you going to tell me what it is?"

"I did get wonderful news, but after the review I'm not certain."

"This is me, Alicia. You can speak freely," Mrs. Bainbridge encouraged. "No one is listening."

"I planned to go to Mr. Caulfield with my new book and make a better agreement. Earlier in the week I received a letter from William Lane Publishing that he was interested in publishing my next story."

Alicia reached into her reticule and removed a folded letter and handed it to Mrs. Bainbridge.

"Mr. Caulfield and I had agreed my next book would be published in February, but we hadn't finalized the contract. When I got to his office, I saw the review. I was disappointed of course, but when he suggested not publishing my story until the summer, I became upset."

Mrs. Bainbridge lifted the quizzing glass that was tied to a ribbon dangling down the front of her bodice and read the letter, while Alicia opened her portmanteau and took out a parcel.

"This is wonderful news." She handed the message back to Alicia.

"William Lane is the biggest publisher in London, if not England. I had offered my books to him before I went to Mr. Caulfield. He said perhaps a smaller shop would be more appropriate for my work and suggested Caulfield Publishing. Isaac Caulfield is a good man, but he maintains tight control over all aspects of my work. I've told him several times I want to be involved. He pats me on the head, tells me not to worry about anything, and sends me on my way. My stories sell well. I planned to ask that we change the contract. I will pay the production costs. He can do the distribution and I would give him a commission based on sales. William Lane will never consider me now, not after reading the review."

Alicia stared unblinking at her friend. She was at a loss for words as Mrs. Bainbridge helped her with her pelisse.

"What makes you imagine Mr. Lane will be different? Be careful what you wish for. A larger company may have more constraints. Now, off with you. And I enjoyed your story. The review was one person's opinion."

"You're right," Alicia said as she jostled her portmanteau and the parcel of books.

"Would it be easier to leave the books in your luggage? The streets ice up in this weather."

"I'm going a short distance and prefer not opening my luggage in the library. I'll manage."

A quick embrace from Mrs. Bainbridge and she was ready to face the weather.

She left the seminary and hadn't gone far before she cursed herself for going at all. The street had turned to mud and ice, and the wind hadn't stopped. Carrying the portmanteau and parcel of books proved to be a more difficult feat than she first imagined.

She crossed the lane and hurried down North Wickham to the library ahead. A dray stood in front of the building on the one area that wasn't muddy. She maneuvered her way around the cart to avoid the large puddles in front of and behind it.

As she reached the door, her feet began to slip on a patch of ice. She juggled the parcel, trying to keep it from falling into the mud. She saved the books, but with the next step her foot slid out from under her. Her hands full, she had no way to stop her fall.

A strong hand grabbed her elbow.

"I've got you," he murmured in her ear.

She caught her balance and looked up into gray eyes that were strikingly familiar, but she had no idea why.

CHAPTER FOUR

"LET ME TAKE those inside for you." The man stood there, his expression openly expectant, as if he knew her. She looked him up and down. He did seem… familiar.

"Have we been introduced, sir?" Alicia asked as he piled her books on top of the ones he carried and opened the door for her.

"I'm Justin—"

"You have my books."

He glanced at what he carried in his arms as if surprised her books were in his hands.

"I do." He gave way and she entered and spotted a stack of her books on a table.

"Please, put mine with the others." She gestured toward the table. "I've come to speak with Mrs. Miller."

The nagging in the back of her mind refused to quiet. She didn't forget a face and his was so distinct, interesting, and… handsome.

"She's not available at the moment." His eyes gleamed with friendly amusement. She was certain she had met him, but where? They moved to the desk at the side of the room.

"Ah, here is her husband. Perhaps he will assist you."

"Captain, the books please." Mr. Miller held out his hand.

Alicia swung around and faced the man. A captain? A flush ran up her neck and colored her cheeks.

"I'm so sorry. You carried my books. When you helped me I…" Stiff, mortified, and rendered momentarily mute, Alicia fought to free her tongue. "Naturally, I thought you worked here at the library."

"Naturally," the captain said, with a devilish look in his eyes.

Did he raise his eyebrow? He thoroughly enjoyed her embarrassment.

"I would have drawn the same conclusion if our positions were reversed." He turned to Mr. Miller. "If you will do the honors."

"By all means. Lady Alicia Hartley, I would like to introduce Captain Justin Caulfield recently of Cameron Highlanders and—"

"It is a pleasure to meet you, Lady Alicia," Justin interrupted.

Her shock slid into suspicion as the memory of strong hands on her shoulders sent a shiver through her. Her pulse quickened at the disturbing thought of who he was.

"Caulfield? I…" She didn't know what to say and worse, what to think.

"This is the second time we've bumped into each other." He tried to control a smile but had little success. "The last time was at my uncle's office."

He leaned close so no one else would hear him but her. "It seems you have a habit of falling into my arms."

Heat radiated from her cheeks. He was flirting with her and the shine in his gaze told her he was enjoying catching her unaware. She rose to the challenge and leaned toward him.

"In London and now here in Sommer-by-the-Sea." She closed her eyes and took a deep breath. "Lavender and citrus. Lovely."

She wasn't through. With a tilt of her head and a sly, playful glance, she touched his arm ever so lightly.

He glanced at once at her hand and back into her eyes. His face went blank with confusion. She wanted to hold the image of that expression.

"I wonder, Captain, who is following whom." Her voice was a whisper.

She reveled in the moment as the shock of her response registered. His soft intake of breath was her undoing. Captain Caulfield graced her with a smile so devastating she thought her heart would stop.

"Touché, Lady Alicia. Going forward I will keep in mind that you have a keen way of retaliating in kind."

Scandalous, but she wasn't the least bit sorry. She was intrigued. Sparring with the captain was almost as good as exchanging words with Effie. No, better. He was pleasant to look at with his longish black hair and silvery gray eyes. She took a deep breath. Lavender and citrus. The lavender should have been soothing, but she knew from now on she would associate the fragrance with the captain being close.

Yes. He was so much better to look at. She could almost taste—

The shameful idea was wicked and reckless. She would have to reprimand herself, but not at the moment.

"Did you have a pleasant journey from London?" he asked.

She pulled her mind away from her errant thoughts and back to reality.

"Yes," she lied. She hated sailing. Although this time she did keep her dinner down. "Did you come all this way simply to deliver my books?"

He paused before he answered.

"My uncle knew I was going to Sommer-by-the-Sea to visit Lord Barrington and asked that I deliver the books. Are you acquainted with His Lordship?"

"Yes. He is a friend of my brother-in-law. They shared a room at Eton. How are you acquainted with Barrington?"

"We served together in Spain," he said.

She almost missed the slight change in his demeanor. His pained expression had her so riddled with guilt that she redirected the line of conversation.

"Do you travel to Sommer-by-the-Sea often? My brother-in-law and Barrington are frequently together with other former military friends." She paused to give him a small smile. "I'm sure I would recall if you were among them."

His posture relaxed and the sparkle returned to his gaze. "This is only my second visit to the village." His direct gaze, focused on her and no one else, held her as close and intimately as if she were in his arms.

Her eyes widened and her heart raced from her chest to her throat, making her breathless.

"Will you be staying long?" For a moment, she was afraid he would say no. Their verbal exchanges were invigorating. She didn't want them to stop.

"I'll be spending the next several weeks with Barrington. The last time we saw each other, you were quite upset with Uncle Isaac. I hope that's been resolved."

Her heart sank at the mention of business. It did put things in their proper perspective. Captain Caulfield was here to see friends and at the library simply to deliver her books. A chance meeting at best. A wave of regret surprised her.

"That remains to be seen." She put a smile on her face and touched her pendant. Her mind quieted. Perhaps she could use this as an opportunity to discuss her grievances.

"Do you write mysteries because you sound—mysterious?" His warm smile and relaxed attitude put her at ease. He wasn't in any rush to end their conversation. He encouraged her to continue. They had only just met, but it was as if they'd known each other a long time.

"Not at all. I write about people who face difficult issues, their journey to resolve them, and how it changes their lives. Some people are not always in accord with the writer."

"I have to agree with you. It's frustrating when someone doesn't understand your characters."

They stood silently for a few moments. Perhaps he was put off speaking about writing with an author, although she thought not. The captain was made of stronger stuff. She wasn't surprised when Mr. Miller mentioned he was a military officer. The vocation fit him. His presence commanded attention and trust.

In his great coat and pure white cravat, much like any other man in the library, he nevertheless stood out from others. Beneath his hat his dark, almost black hair was short and romantically wild. His longish sideburns framed a handsome face. His gray eyes held, no commanded, one's attention. His stature and striking good looks were a dangerous combination.

"Your characters, Captain?"

"Yes. Like you, I'm an author. My stories are about my experiences in the service."

She nodded, feigning interest. Several of Elkington's friends had penned their stories and, may the lord forgive her, she suffered through reading their work looking for something complimentary to say. The men wrote from their heart, but their books would be of little interest to anyone other than the author and possibly his loved ones.

"You have no interest in military stories."

She tilted her head toward him. Was her veneer so easy to detect?

"I have read the accounts of service men. They tell what happened without any reaction. In more cases than I want to admit, it sounds like a list of actions without any thinking or emotions."

"Yes. I've read stories like that. I find myself yawning as I read them. However, in most cases I understand what the author is trying to say. The value is in the men letting out their stories. They use their minds to bring back the event, their hands and fingers to write them down so it is not forgotten, and in the end, they give their soul relief."

It was her turn to be surprised. There was no question about his caring. She stared past the handsome trappings and found a man of depth and passion. A man she wanted to learn more about.

"The gruesomeness of what the men went through must have been difficult to write. How was I so unfeeling not to see their pain? I read it as fiction and not as a means of dispelling their demons." With all her heart she felt for these men. She touched the captain's sleeve. "I hope they were successful and found the peace they sought."

He put his hand over hers and patted it gently. He said nothing for a few heartbeats. His silent gratitude was enough.

"My characters tackle different issues. I write about women fighting in a society where they are expected to run a house and bear children and are unjustly punished for their intelligence and breaking society's rules, no matter how minor. Many a woman rots away from lack of direction, affection, and never finds the true meaning of her life. My stories are for those women.

"My stories are about women who use whatever is needed to find solutions, take action, protect those they love."

"That *is* a challenge," he nodded, encouraging her to go on, "your own war of sorts." His full attention didn't waver.

Yes. Her heroines did fight their own battles. The intelligence of his observation and the intensity of his attention encouraged her to go on.

"My heroine bends the rules, but she is not the difficult character to write."

"That leaves your hero. What do you find most challenging about writing characters of the opposite sex?" he asked.

Startled by his question, she lifted her head and stared at him. Had he read the *Gazette's* review?

"I ask because I've been accused of not doing justice to my female characters." His tone held a note of regret.

If his question startled her, his open honest reason humbled her.

"You pose an interesting question. It isn't easy writing a character who isn't…you."

The clock on the mantel struck the hour.

The captain looked at the timepiece. When he turned to her, he didn't appear pleased.

"I've enjoyed our talk and I'd like to continue our discussion at length. I regret I must leave. I'm expected at Lord Barrington's."

"We must meet. I would hate to leave your question unanswered." Was that too forward?

"As would I." His low mellow voice sent a delightful shiver up her spine.

"Have you seen much of Sommer-by-the-Sea?"

He shook his head.

"If you like, I'll take you for a tour."

"What a delightful solution. Are you available tomorrow afternoon?"

"Yes. I am. Why don't we meet here?" If he was startled that she didn't suggest meeting her at home, he didn't show it.

"Until tomorrow." He touched the brim of his hat, and with a swirl of his great coat he headed for the door. He glanced over his shoulder at her before he opened it, gave her a nod, and was gone.

The tinkling of the silver bell broke her out of the spell he had cast.

"The captain is gone," one of the clerks said as she finished adding books to the table and stood back. "I have *The Lost Dowry* and *In My Brother's Shadow* all ready."

Alicia inspected the table and looked at the books in horror.

"*In My Brother's...*" She turned to the clerk. "Why on earth are those books with mine?"

"With both authors here, Mr. Miller couldn't pass up the opportunity to have them read for our patrons." The woman adjusted the books, enabling patrons who entered to find them.

"No. Of course not," she whispered under her breath.

"Mr. Miller asked that I tell you he has had to change the schedule. The reading is moved to Tuesday. He hopes that isn't inconvenient."

For a moment she saw a way to avoid the uncomfortable situation. As fast as the idea surfaced, she dashed it. J. C. Melrose wasn't going to make her cower.

"Not at all. Tuesday is fine."

The clerk nodded and left her by the table which was just as well.

Why was she upset? The event was a reading. All she had to do was read a scene, answer a few questions, and sign bookplates. That won't be so difficult. She rubbed her pendant and let out a calming breath.

Alicia looked at the sturdy leather cover of the Melrose book. Was the hero, Captain Mallory worthy of her Clarissa? Effie thought so.

Read his story and make your own decision.

Effie and Mr. Lindsay may be right. She should understand her enemy. Alicia picked up the Melrose book and read the first few pages. She closed the cover, her heart pounding. She found a comfortable chair near the hearth and spent the next few hours devouring the book.

The fighting was explicit. Some scenes shocked her, but she read on. Other scenes made her smile, even laugh. There were scenes that brought her to tears. She kept reading, unable to put the book down.

Daylight dwindled. The clerk lit the lanterns. She never read a book twice, but this one was more than a story. This book was inspiration. She went to the desk and purchased it.

How was anyone able to breathe such life into a hero and make him jump off the page? Several times she found herself looking toward the door waiting for Captain Mallory to enter the library and seek her out. By the end of the second chapter, she more than cared about him, she wanted to fight at his side.

"Lady Alicia," Mrs. Miller approached her. "I didn't want to bother you while you were reading. I'm sorry I wasn't available when you arrived."

"Your husband took good care of me."

"You've read *In My Brother's Shadow*. I enjoyed it. Did you?"

Alicia covered her uneasiness with what she hoped was a pleasant smile. Anxieties about her book ran rampant in her mind. Perhaps she should claim she was unavailable on Tuesday. Once the reading was over and everyone had heard both authors' selections, they would know Lady Alicia Hartley was not an author, but an imposter, and a poor one at that.

"Charles told me *In My Brother's Shadow* is precise in capturing the personal struggles. The descriptions brought him back to the battlefield. The reading should be exciting."

"Yes, I enjoyed the story from the first word until the last."

"Now, your Clarissa. She is everything I want to be, independent, clever, and yet works within most of the limits set by society. I'm looking forward to your reading, as are many of our patrons. I'm never disappointed with your stories. Are you aware of the change in our schedule?"

"Yes. The reading is on Tuesday. Mrs. Miller, thank you for the invitation. Until then."

"Don't forget our annual Harvest Salon on Tuesday evening."

"I wouldn't miss it."

Alicia thanked her and left the shop. On her way home she couldn't help wondering how J. C. Melrose included so much emotion on every page. She was curious to find out the secret to such writing. Perhaps then she'd have the answer to the captain's question.

What do I find most difficult about writing characters of the opposite sex?

CHAPTER FIVE

JUSTIN SAT WITH Barrington and the other retired officers in the library at Sommer Chase, Barrington's townhouse on the Sommer River. He turned the establishment into a private men's club of sorts. It was a place where he and his close friends met, exercised, and deliberated without interruption.

Injured in battle getting his men out of harm's way, Barrington was not expected to walk again. His immobility was an irritation, one he wouldn't accept. No one was surprised by his determination. He had taught them how to face unsurmountable odds and not retreat until every option and tactic was exhausted. He faced his injury with the same determination.

Justin and the others rallied to help him. The man was so much more than their commanding officer. He encouraged, consoled, scolded, and created a team that was the envy of everyone, even Wellington. *Loyalty* was the word that summed him up. He had not abandoned them on the battlefield. His officers would not abandon him when he needed them most.

While he recuperated in London at Barrington Hall, his friends worked together and turned the ballroom into an exercise room. Each man helped him exercise and train. As he had kept up their morale while they convalesced, they did the same for him.

Last year, Barrington called Justin and the others to Sommer-by-the-Sea. As the men waited in the drawing room, their former commanding officer made his entrance walking into the room with his mother on his arm. Everyone jumped to their feet, shouting and applauding his success. Justin still felt the excitement and accomplishment of that day.

Exercising helped both Barrington's mind and body. He wasn't going to end his rehabilitation and risk regressing. He had a need to accomplish more. At the root of it, he did not want to lose the camaraderie with his men. They had a deep strong bond.

Barrington's father stood with him proud and happy after he walked into the room with his mother.

"With gratitude and humility, Lady Barrington and I thank you for all you have done. We never thought our son would walk again. He was right when he told me his men perform miracles. Please accept this small token as a remembrance of our gratitude." Lord Barrington signaled the butler, and a small box was presented to each man.

"Every man in our family is given a coin, a talisman of sorts. The custom has been handed down for centuries. It began as a way of identifying the carrier as an emissary from the family. While its use is obsolete, the tradition has continued. This coin has been made especially for you, the men of The League and signifies you are part of a unique group."

They opened each small box. Inside they found a gold coin embossed with a circle of laurel leaves. Within the circle were the letters, TLS.

"Gentlemen." Everyone turned to their former commander.

He raised his glass. "To you, the men of The League of Sommer-by-the-Sea."

They toasted together.

Now, Justin sat with his friends. He didn't concentrate on the conversation about French brandy and smugglers. Ah, but Alasdair Lawson, his cousin on his mother's side – there was still a hint of the free trader about him. He kept Barrington and several others in fine brandy.

His mind was elsewhere, specifically on Alicia. The woman fascinated him. From his uncle's ravings about his prize author, he expected someone entirely different, more…passive and perhaps malleable.

No. She wasn't vapid or boring in the least. Intelligent, outspoken, if perhaps a bit clumsy at times, but that made her charming. She was strong and determined, a bluestocking with a trace of uncertainty thrown in to make her human.

Her writing would reflect her personality. Her heroine more than passed the test according to a portion of the *Gazette* review. But her hero and supporting characters fell short. Is that why his uncle wanted him to read her stories?

Working through plot points, conflicts, resolutions and developing characters together could be productive, possibly enjoyable. Their discussions would be charged and could lead to better works for both of them. He couldn't imagine them ever being dull.

For a moment, he vividly saw Alicia sitting at a large table across from him, deep in thought. Every now and then they would talk through some point or character issue. He could imagine the flush of excitement on her cheeks.

The image faded and left him empty. He was beginning to understand his uncle's enthusiasm about her. No matter which direction he took with his writing career, he owed it to his uncle to ensure she continued to publish with Caulfield Publishing. It wouldn't be a burden. He'd be doing it for his uncle, for the company.

"Justin? Justin. You haven't heard a word we've said."

Startled from his reverie, he straightened in his chair. "No. Forgive me, my mind wandered."

"Conjuring a new plot, I suspect. We should all be alert," Simon Watts said. "I've never seen a genius at work."

"You still haven't," Peter Simms said as they laughed.

"I would be careful if I were you. Those remarks can get you killed." Justin's icy stare quieted the group. "In my next story and in the most agonizing way."

The group laughed louder.

"Now, what were you saying about French brandy?" he asked as he leaned forward.

⟫⟫⟫❮❮❮

THE FOLLOWING DAY the wind had almost worn itself out. The rain clouds moved out to sea. The sun was shining, giving the village a welcome respite from bad weather. Intermittent gusts of wind whipped down the village lanes, catching the edges of Alicia's pelisse and threatening to pull her hat loose. Alicia and her sister Beatrice hurried along and made their way to Mrs. Miller's.

"The sun feels good after a week of rain. You chose a good day to tour the village with Captain Caulfield. Should we ask him to dine with us?" Her sister's mischievous smile irritated her.

"We need not go that far. You used the same tactic with Commander Terrell. You are worse than Mother." The more she brought to light about the captain, the more her sister would pester her. Alicia let out a deep breath.

"Regarding the captain, I'm not sure if his uncle sent him here or if it is a coincidence he's visiting Lord Barrington. I suppose I'll never know. But it does have me curious. Anyway, I'm glad you're joining me."

"I will admit I was surprised you invited me. Elkington almost choked on his sherry last night. It seems we've gotten accustomed to you galivanting around on your own."

"That is a turn of events, you both being shocked." In spite of herself, Alicia chuckled. "I asked for a companion rather than traumatizing you to find me wandering without one. Let's not tell Mother and Father. I wouldn't want them to think I've reformed."

"No, let's not..." Beatrice looked at the sky. "Do you think the weather will hold?"

"If you believe the *Old Moore's Almanack* prediction, the

weather will remain good until tomorrow. The publication stated the uncommon rain would be followed by sea storms and tides higher than usual. Others must believe the almanac is correct." Alicia gestured toward the dock.

The harbor was alive with activity. Ships arriving on the morning tide filled the docks. Stevedores were busy unloading the ships and moving the cargo to safety indoors as quickly as possible. No one wanted to lose goods to the bad weather.

"You've never shown anyone about the village before. What made you decide to start with Captain Caulfield?" Her sister bit the side of her cheek trying to keep a straight face.

"He's my publisher's nephew. Why do you ask?" She waited for Beatrice's answer. Her poor sister could not reply. She must be out of practice.

Alicia hurried her steps, eager to speak to the captain. Unable to sleep for numerous reasons, one of which were haunting gray eyes, she spent the evening laying in her bed in deep thought. She only fell asleep once she had her answer to yesterday's question.

They crossed the square and came to the library. The small silver bell at the top of the door tinkled, notifying the librarian of the sisters' arrival. The room was busy with people browsing the shelves. A table near the desk was stacked with a handbill about the particulars of the forthcoming reading event.

Join us for Tea and Tales
Tuesday, 15 November at four of-the-clock
This month, two distinguished authors read from their
recent works about sacrifice and loyalty
Lady Alicia Hartley's highly praised story *The Lost Dowry*
introduces us to a young woman who uses her dowry to save
her family
and

J. C. Melrose's acclaimed book *In My Brother's Shadow* is the
story of a man who takes his battle-damaged brother's place
in the army.

"You didn't tell me there was another author reading with you," her sister said, speaking in an odd yet gentle tone.

Alicia straightened herself. "Why bother you or Elkington with something so inconsequential?"

"Perhaps because of late, this author appears to be the bane of your existence." Beatrice's eyes held a lethal calmness.

Thank the lord, the metallic tinkle of a bell saved her from having to continue the conversation.

She didn't need the tiny bell to be aware Captain Caulfield had entered. Her heart pounded so loud she was sure he could hear it across the room.

He stood at the door in his great coat and hat like any other man, but he appeared more striking. He spoke with Mr. Miller. Every so often he glanced in her direction, dipped his head ever so slightly and sent her heart racing.

She took a steadying breath and turned to Beatrice, who had busied herself.

By all that was holy. Her own sister had picked up *In My Brother's Shadow* and was reading it.

"Traitor," she whispered for Beatrice's ears.

"I thought you said he was inconsequential?" Her sister chuckled and kept on reading. "This is quite good. You should read it."

She imagined strangling her sister on the spot. It was only thoughts of Elkington's grief that stopped her. Theirs was a love match, the type she hoped for. They had their differences, but they would work it out.

"Good day, Lady Alicia." The captain stood in front of her, his eyes compelling and magnetic.

Alicia found it impossible not to return his captivating smile.

"Captain Caulfield. Let me introduce you to my sister, Lady Beatrice Elkington."

"Pleased, I'm sure, my lady." He tipped his head and gave Beatrice his full attention. "Lady Alicia mentioned you are married to Captain Douglas Elkington?"

"Why, yes. Are you acquainted with my husband?" Beatrice asked.

Alicia looked on in amazement, caught off guard by Beatrice's question.

"We both served with Lord Barrington." A proud smile broadened on his face.

"You must be a member of Barrington's League."

In these last two years her brother-in-law never once mentioned any connection to Caulfield. She started digging into her memory. She returned from speaking with Mr. Lane about publishing her first book and gave Beatrice and Elkington all the ugly facts. *Now* she recalled. Not only did William Lane suggest she speak to Isaac Caulfield, but Elkington had, as well. Was her brother-in-law more involved in getting her books published than only suggesting she speak to the publisher?

The captain raised his head and glanced at Lady Elkington. "Yes, I am."

"Now I'm doubly pleased to meet you. My sister mentioned you will be in Sommer-by-the-Sea for several weeks. You must call on us."

Dipping his head he said, "You're most gracious, Lady Elkington."

"Now, if you will excuse me." She turned to Alicia. "I have a few errands I must see to. Why don't you take Captain Caulfield for a tour of the cathedral, and I'll meet you at home? You promised to go over the plans for the Harvest Party."

Before Alicia could respond to her sister's sudden exit, the little silver bell tinkled as she went out the door. Elkington was not going to get away with conveniently neglecting to tell her why he never mentioned his relationship with the Caulfields.

"Does she do that often?" The captain stared at the door. "Perhaps we should escape before she changes her mind and returns."

She looked at him, first in surprise. Then she shook her head, laughing.

"No?" His feigned disappointment was comical. "I suppose the cathedral it is. Shall we?" He offered her his arm.

"You never told me you knew Elkington," she said as they started toward the door.

"I hadn't thought about it." He brought them to a halt. "Is it important?"

"I suppose it isn't." Unless her brother-in-law conspired with Caulfield to publish her stories. Did it matter? She let out a deep sigh. Her books were published, and people bought them. *That* was all that mattered.

They left the library, walked along Wickham and across Westmore Commons. He listened with interest as she pointed out various places.

They had a pleasant time. She didn't mind giving him a local history lesson but wanted to continue yesterday's discussion.

"That's Sommer Castle," she said, indicating the building on the hill to their left.

They turned up Cathedral Court and headed toward the cathedral with its fine tower.

"You use your real name on your books," he said.

"Yes. There is no need for me to obscure who I am. Although, it did ignite a heated discussion within the family when I presented them with my first published book." She turned and innocently smiled. "By then it was too late."

"I found it necessary to use my—"

"I've been thinking about your question," she interrupted but looked straight ahead as they walked.

He said nothing.

"You asked what I found most difficult about writing characters of the opposite sex."

Alicia glanced at him from the corner of her eye. He focused straight ahead. She wasn't sure of his expression.

"You have an answer?" He glanced at her. His brow raised.

"Yes, I do." She let out a deep breath and grabbed her courage. "In writing a character, you need to understand how they think and react. First, the author needs to understand men and women don't react in the same way."

After practicing *that* for at least an hour last night, she was pleased with her delivery.

"I understand. Men, as the stronger of the two, are intelligent, courageous, and determined. Women, on the other hand are governed by their emotions and their virtues. They are expected to be chaste, modest, and pious." He turned and faced her. "Do you agree?"

"No. I believe your view of women is…" She countered icily, then stopped, silently counting to ten. That was not the path of reasoning, if one could call that reasoning, she expected him to take. This man may be her publisher's nephew, but that didn't stop her from wanting to hit him with anything she could find. In truth, she was disappointed. She let out a breath and started again, this time in better control.

"Incorrect. That may be all you see but there is much more to a woman that drives her actions and reactions."

His brow wrinkled and their pace slowed.

"Men are quiet and focus on the task at hand," he said. "They are not distracted with emotions but take direct action."

"Yes, I agree." Encouraged he was listening, she went on. "To you…quiet and focused, to a woman…isolated and controlled. Men are all about fixing the problem and not thinking about it to determine what needs fixing."

"And women? Are you saying they are not emotional?" he asked, not trying to hide his confusion.

"Women are an instinctive and a sensitive lot. We listen, then react and yes, we respond to tone and emotions. Our reaction is based on our responsibility within the family. Keeping peace, order, and safety are meant to be paramount to us. We're supposed to be good at working with and organizing groups, talking with them, focusing on a solution that works for everyone in the group."

"Men are sensitive," he said with a strand of defense in his tone. "We react to a woman's emotions."

"When Beatrice was upset, Elkington did react. He left the room." She stopped, closed her eyes, mortified at her blunder, and touched his arm.

Justin stopped. He looked at her and glanced at her hand on his arm. She withdrew it and he dragged his gaze up to her face.

"Please, don't mention what I said to either of them."

He gave her a smile that took her breath away. He bent toward her, his lips almost touching her ear.

"Your secret is safe. But I may ask for a boon."

She nodded, breathless. "And if I refuse?" she said.

"You will leave me no alternative; I will blackmail you, of course."

She enjoyed his gentle sparring as much as he did. "I can't let that happen, can I." It was hard for her to keep from smiling.

He pulled her arm through his and continued on. "Good. It is forgotten. Yes, men do react, but our instinct is to resolve the issue. We put great thought into the problem and decide what is best for the woman. It may not be what she wants."

"Exactly my point. Men *imagine* they know what is best for the woman and what she wants—"

"Are you saying they don't?" he interrupted.

"They don't, but nonetheless, they make the decision without discussing or consulting with her."

"And that's what a woman wants, to be consulted?"

She glanced at his face as they continued on. Deep lines of concentration appeared along his brows and under his eyes.

"Do you like it when decisions are made that impact you without care for the consequences? All in the guise that it is the right action, of course. All done for your own good."

They arrived outside the cathedral. He stopped, knew exactly what she meant. There were times when orders were given that he thought…well, that wasn't the issue right now. But in dealing with women?

"Women are better at discussing and sharing information.

They can talk through issues with others to arrive at a resolution that best serves the group."

He still considered the issue. "If that is true, how should Elkington have responded to your sister?"

"With comfort and compassion. They should talk about the issue and reach an agreement, together."

He chuckled and gazed at the square church tower. "Men are not known for their compassion. If we speak about the expected roles of men and women, then the man is the provider and protector. When he is faced with a situation, it is his primary responsibility to protect those at risk."

Alicia nodded. "I hadn't thought about the differences between men and women in those terms. Men focus on risk and women strive on managing the group, the young, the family."

She understood her hero and heroine would approach solving a problem differently but hadn't realized why. The man was responding the way he knew how, taking action, taking control. The hero's growth would come from understanding and developing a working relationship with the heroine. And vice versa.

Her excitement built as scenes in her new story came to mind. She knew they needed to be rewritten, but how?

Isaac told her she had a tendency to overlook the natural struggles between her hero and heroine. Now it became clear.

"This difference could have the hero and heroine thinking differently about everything," she said more to herself. Yes, that made perfect sense to her. Beatrice's private discussion sprang into her mind. "Even intimacy."

"I beg your pardon." He dropped his voice to a low raspy whisper, sending chills down her spine. A sly smile brightened his face.

Alicia, her face flushed with heat, wanted to melt into the stones. And in front of the cathedral.

"For women, intimacy starts in their head, not necessarily…" Her face was so hot she was going to go up in flames.

"Oh, really?"

If she thought his soft, mellow voice or his smoldering stare couldn't get any more suggestive, she was wrong.

"I'm an author. I write about relationships and emotions," she replied, unable to face him.

"And intimacy," he purred.

She closed her eyes and tried not to think about how her body was responding to his suggestions. Was he suggesting…inviting?

"Please forgive me, Lady Alicia. I've carried our conversation into topics that in the present company should not be spoken. It was playful banter for which I apologize. If you prefer, I'll bring you home."

"No," she snapped, turning to face him. "I mean you're forgiven, Captain. I am equally responsible. I diverted our conversation into subjects not appropriate to discuss in your company."

Her fingers itched to push away the lock of hair that fell boyishly over his forehead. Instead, she stood and stared at him.

"A shared culpability." He let out a breath and smiled. "Why don't you tell me about the cathedral?"

Relieved, she faced the building. He did the same.

"The cathedral was founded in 1091, the same time as Sommer Castle. A great fire destroyed the cathedral in 1216. It took over 130 years to be rebuilt. The tower with its lantern spire is one of the most beautiful of its type. It was added in the early 1400s and was the main navigation point for ships using the Sommer River.

"The tower saved the city from invasion. If no', I would have been speaking tae ye like a Scotswoman."

He squeezed his eyes shut and scrunched his shoulders. She was aware her attempt at a Scottish accent was laughable. At least he *was* laughing.

"Ye dinnae have it right, lassie. Ye should no' try what yer no' capable of doing."

She stared at him.

"My grandparents on my mother's side are from—"

"They're from Scotland," she interrupted.

"Yes, my mother is part of—"

"One of my characters was a lass from Edinburgh."

THE CLAN MELROSE. That's what he started to say. On second thought, her interruption was fortunate. He didn't want to divert a very pleasant conversation. He'd have to find a more opportune time. At the moment, he preferred to learn more about the cathedral's history.

"How did the tower prevent you from acquiring a fine Scottish brogue?"

"It was during a nine-week siege by Scottish invaders in 1644. They made all sorts of demands. But the people wouldn't agree to any of them. There were skirmishes and fights. Your ancestors, forgive me Captain, but they were not a nice lot, stole the grain and scared the livestock so there was no milk from the cows or eggs from the chickens. The villagers fought back valiantly and took prisoners."

"It's an unfortunate part of war," he said softly.

"The invaders took whatever they wanted and when there was nothing left to take, they demanded more. They wanted gold. But the mayor stood firm. The only item of value in the cathedral was the treasured chalice. He wouldn't surrender the relic."

"So how did the tower save the good people of Sommer-by-the-Sea?" he asked.

"Patience, I'm coming to that." She placed her hand on his arm.

Her brief touch made him more aware of her standing at his side than he wanted to admit. Her playful banter charmed him.

He enjoyed her tale, and her telling even more.

She leaned in as if she told him the greatest secret. Her large hazel eyes grew bigger when she spoke, and her smile sparkled. He found himself hanging on her every word.

"The Scottish men who came here, not your direct forbearers I'm sure, threatened if the mayor didn't give them the gold chalice, they would bombard the tower. Gold? There was no gold chalice, especially in the 1600s. The relic's value was in what it symbolized in the religious ritual, not the substance of which it was made. But I digress. The attackers made their threat, and our mayor Sir John Whitaker developed a plan." She lowered her voice, intriguing him even more.

"Your forbearers suffered their losses. I'm sorry to tell you some lost their lives and others, well, they became guests of the mayor. He provided quarters for them at Sommer Castle, in the dungeon, deep underground.

"The deeper they went into the ground, the greater the stink of wet, pungent mildew. Black mold grew across the walls and parts of the floor. Despite the smell, they were forced to go on. At the bottom, they came to a door. The door opened onto what appeared to be a stone forest, a broad, pillared hall with stone columns as large as tree trunks."

"It sounds frightening." Her eyes twinkled as she artfully painted the picture with words. The story enchanted him, but not as much as the enchantress.

"The dungeon was horrifying. Thick cobwebs filled the corners of the room. Wisps of webbing hung from the ceiling and waved in the stale air. The room held a curious array of tools. Winches and levers projected from every wall, and chains with handles dangled from the ceiling. Manacles were set into the walls. One set of manacles was broken open. This is where the men were held."

Alicia's voice had taken on a lost, distant sound reminding him of men who relived their battlefield experiences. His concern grew to alarm. Strong men had crumbled under less.

"When were you there last?" he asked as he gently took her hand.

"I haven't been there in many years."

He lifted her chin with the crook of his finger. The urge to kiss her was all-consuming. He wanted to kiss away the pained expression in her eyes and bring back the warm smile to her now pale face.

Instead, they spoke not a word and let their eyes convey what they couldn't. Slowly, her pained expression receded. Her pale face replaced with a warm smile. He removed his hand.

She had immersed herself in the scene and taken him along with her.

"The dungeon is open to visitors." She let out a deep breath but didn't move away. "It is also the prison where Judge Scofield sends someone too dangerous to keep in the village jail. I don't remember him ever giving that order. Barrington saw the dungeon about three years ago when the young Rogers boy was missing."

"Was he in the dungeon?" He gave her a worried glance.

"No, he was hiding from his mother in their barn. No one wants to be in the dungeon during the day. The boy was missing all night. Even he didn't want to be down there alone."

"Clever boy." He nodded at the boy's good sense. "What was the fate of my Scottish brethren?"

"In the middle of the night the mayor had all the Scottish prisoners put in the tower. Your forebearers are a loyal bunch and wouldn't risk their brethren's lives. The siege ended in a truce. The prisoners were released on the condition they do not return. That is how the cathedral tower saved me from having a Scottish brogue."

"And I apologize for the error of my forebearers' ways. But they did add some color to your history."

She couldn't control her burst of laughter and he joined her in sincere amusement.

They spent the remainder of their time examining the cathedral's stained-glass windows before they started back to Hartmore Manor.

"We'll walk along the river. You'll have a good view of the castle from there. Well, you'll have a good view of the castle from just about everywhere. It sits on a promontory. Perhaps tomorrow we'll explore it, if you'd like."

"That's kind of you, Lady Alicia. I would enjoy seeing the castle with you."

They hadn't walked far when Alicia stopped.

"Is something amiss?"

He looked into her eyes and saw true concern.

"No, Captain Caulfield. I enjoyed our conversation about…characters and their differences."

"If I offended you, I'm sorry." He took her hand and brought it to his lips. "That was not my intent."

Her tender expression hit him hard. Hard enough that his heart skipped a beat.

"Not at all," she said, her voice low and breathless. "Nor was it mine."

CHAPTER SIX

THE SOUNDS OF jabs, counterpunches, hooks and upper cuts finding their mark along with the grunts of both men echoed in the large room in Sommer Chase. Justin and Barrington spent the morning in the exercise room sparring. For Barrington, it was therapeutic. For Justin, it was a release of anxieties and even some guilt. He exploded with a barrage of punches.

"Hold," Barrington shouted.

Justin, preparing to deliver another jab, held up. Sweat dampened his shirt. He was breathing hard. He dropped his arms and followed his friend to the side of the room.

"You've always been an aggressive boxer. It's the reason I enjoy sparring with you. However, I don't remember the last time you were this driven," Barrington said, offering him a towel.

"I have a great deal on my mind." Justin put the gloves away and draped the towel around his neck.

"I'm listening."

"I'll tell you when I have it sorted out." What would Barrington think of him if he suspected he even contemplated being disloyal to his uncle. The other League members would have similar opinions. But his commander would not let it go, better he changed the subject. "You want to talk about Edinburgh."

Barrington hesitated. As his friend weighed his next words, Justin hoped he would move on and not press him for an answer.

"Alasdair Lawson sent word asking for you." Barrington let out a chuckle. "He told me not to bother sending anyone else. Why is that?"

Justin gave him a crooked smile.

"Ale. I hold mine better than you. He can drink longer with me. You, my friend, fall asleep at the table." Justin couldn't help but laugh. The last time the three of them were together, Barrington was asleep before he and his cousin got started.

"Ale? Is that what you call the swill he drinks?" The humor died down and Barrington became serious. "Lawson said he has information about the smugglers. They risk the treacherous tides and use the caves along our coast where they hide from the Sea and Land Guard. Like other coastal towns and villages, they have plied the locals with money and goods, making them allies. Now people find it difficult to discern who is friend and who is foe. Lawson has information we need. The situation is tense, so take care."

"I'm leaving in the morning." He slipped on his coat, leaving it open.

"This should give you a story or two for your next book." They left the exercise room and headed for the staircase. "Where are you off to today?"

"Lady Alicia has made it her goal to educate me about Sommer-by-the-Sea. Today we are exploring the castle."

"There is little left of the palace. Shops and houses have been built on the castle grounds, but it has a proud history. I'll have the carriage ready for you."

"There is no need."

"Nonsense. Lady Alicia is a lovely woman. Elkington is her brother-in-law."

"I wasn't aware of the connection when we met. I won't hold it against her."

"She is headstrong and outspoken. I can see where your common interests would draw you to each other."

"I'm not looking for an attachment." That was the last thing he needed. He had a vow to keep. "Not until I've taken care of the Frenchman."

He stood there, his hands cramping in fists, his jaw muscle twitching, seeing another time. "He used Matthew. I never should have left without him when I returned to London with you and Wellington."

"Matthew was a seasoned soldier," Barrington said softly.

"It's my fault Matthew was vulnerable." Didn't Barrington realize, everyone around him was in jeopardy.

Captured in a skirmish, he was surprised when Napoleon came to the camp specifically to meet him, "the great Highland warrior." The little emperor's prize.

"My man here doesn't think very highly of you, Captain," Napoleon said. "If you are this great Highland warrior, how is it you are my prisoner?"

Justin looked from the Frenchmen to Napoleon and smiled. "Fifty of my men were in the skirmish. My detail suffered no casualties, and I am your only captive," he said in his best Scottish brogue. "Why is that?"

Napoleon's expression morphed from excessive pride to admiration.

"You sacrificed yourself for your men." The Corsican opened the little shell box he carried that was filled with slivers of licorice flavored with aniseed. The emperor of France offered a piece to Justin.

Justin stared at the man as a silent respect passed between them. He graciously accepted the offered treat.

Napoleon nodded at Justin's acceptance. He put the small box away without offering any to his man. Justin could feel the tension in the room grow. If Napoleon felt it, he said and did nothing. Instead, he pulled a book out of his pocket.

"Have you read James Macpherson's translation of Ossian? I find this book arouses my strongest passions."

"I enjoy his poetry," Justin said.

The man's eyes lit. "Ah, a kindred soul. You're not only a warrior, but a man of passion and great literature."

"I can see why the story of Ossian attracts you. It rejects the superiority of the civilized society and its culture in favor of the natural, wild

and primitive. The story seeks heroic meaning in the culture of the people of the past."

"Yes, precisely," Napoleon said eagerly and took a seat in front of his captive.

The Corsican turned to his henchman. "And you? Do you enjoy reading?"

His henchman said nothing.

"I thought not. Leave us." He waved his man away.

"But sir—"

Napoleon abruptly turned and stared at the man without saying a word.

The Frenchman stared long and hard at Justin. A satanic smile spread across his thin lips before he nodded to his emperor and left.

"He would not understand." Napoleon let out a deep breath as the tent flap closed. "He is an odd one. In my eagerness to talk to you about your fellow Scotsman, I have created a problem for you. He does not take well to being anything other than the most important person." He leaned close to Justin. "There are times I worry for my own well-being." That made the man chuckle as he sat back. "I would be cautious, especially around him."

Several hours later, after sharing brandy and discussing Macpherson as well as other classics, Napoleon walked him to the edge of the encampment.

"I hope you enjoyed the evening as much as I have," Napoleon said. "I give you a boon. We will stand back-to-back then walk. I will return to my men, and you will return to yours."

Justin wasn't prepared. He was ready to fight for his life. He never imagined Napoleon would let him leave alive.

He nodded. Said nothing. Stayed on high alert. Turned and felt the heat of Napoleon's back on his.

They both started walking. With each step he waited for the sound of a musket. He kept moving forward as he entered the woods. It wasn't until he saw Matthew that he finally looked back. Through the trees he watched Napoleon enter his tent.

At the edge of the camp stood a lone figure. The Frenchman.

"Come quickly," Matthew said as he pulled Justin along. "It's a long way to camp. What happened?"

Justin kept moving. "I've made a very powerful enemy and it wasn't Napoleon."

"Matthew's death was not your fault," Barrington said.

"You didn't see the revenge in the Frenchmen's eyes as I did. Napoleon warned me." The man would use anyone to make him regret those two hours with Napoleon.

The Frenchman's reputation preceded him. Barrington and Wellington were aware that Justin was the man's prime target. But the man was a master of disguise. No one knew who the Frenchman was. It was what made the man Napoleon's greatest asset.

"The Frenchman was very convincing. Under the guise of a French revolutionary, Jacque, the man established a close friendship with Matthew while I was in London.

"When I returned to the camp, *Jacque* was all Matthew could talk about. The two dined together, drank together, talked about their families, and what the future would hold.

"He specifically chose Matthew, no one else," Justin said. "What he didn't know was Matthew was as much a Highland warrior as me. He had gone to meet Jacque and walked into a trap."

Barrington didn't say anything. The commander knew Justin had to let it out.

"When we found him, he was still alive. He gave me a message from the Frenchman before he died. 'Tell the great Highland warrior I'm sending you back to say good-bye.'"

"But that wasn't what kept him alive," Barrington reminded him. "In all his pain, he laughed telling the two of us he gave his torturer wrong information about the troop positions in Salamanca. It was what helped us win the battle. He was a great Highland warrior to the end."

Justin turned to Barrington. "Don't you see? He singled out Matthew because of me. Anyone I am attached to would be in jeopardy."

"Do you think this vendetta is real? His threat is just his sick way of playing with your mind."

Justin stood at the bottom of the staircase and turned to him. "His threat is very real. I've pursued him as best I can. I think we're safe for the moment while he's with his emperor. He'll leave Napoleon's side and when he does, I will find him."

"You won't give up this mission? Not even for Lady Alicia?" Barrington asked.

He cleared his throat. "Lady Alicia *is* all the things you say. She is interesting, creative, and mysterious. I enjoy her company. I find myself thinking about her at the oddest moments. She has qualities I never thought I'd find, never thought I would want to look for."

"My friend, you may not be looking for an attachment, but it sounds like you've found one." Barrington chuckled as they climbed to the second floor.

They reached the top of the stairs. Barrington stopped and turned toward him.

"I admire your loyalty. Not only to Matthew, but to all the men, and to me. But it doesn't stop with being loyal to others. You must be loyal to yourself. You can't cut yourself off from the world. It leaves you little to fight for. You and the other League members taught me that lesson." Barrington stared at him, his concern evident. "Lady Alicia may be worth fighting for. Have a good trip and drink a round of that swill for me."

Justin stood looking after his friend as Barrington walked to his room. He more than anyone understood loyalty and the need to finish a mission. The man's words weighed heavy with him. Barrington had never led him astray. He was more conflicted than ever before.

IT WAS A short ride to Hartmore Manor on the other side of the

Sommer River.

Determined to quell his building anxiety, he planned to speak to Elkington and explain his dilemma. Not about publishing with William Lane. That had become less important to him than telling Alicia his author's identity.

The carriage pulled up to the manor. Ready to get the deed over with, he got out of the carriage, stood at the door, and pulled the bell cord.

"Good day, Captain Caulfield. Lady Alicia is expecting you. This way please."

"Is Captain Elkington at home?"

"No, sir."

He wasn't sure if he was relieved or vexed. He didn't have much time to resolve his dilemma. The butler ushered him into the drawing room.

"Captain Caulfield," he announced and quietly disappeared.

Alicia stood by the mantel. She had a twisted handkerchief in her hand. Her face was radiant and flushed. Her lips were damp, parted, and inviting.

He looked away and let out an incomprehensible, awkward cough. He forced himself to find her sister who sat daintily on the settee with a book in her hand.

His heart skipped a beat when he realized she was reading his book. This was worse than he imagined. How did they find out? Elkington must have told them. What did that matter now? All he could do was take the blows whatever they would be.

Quickly going through possible outcomes, he froze at the possibility of Alicia never speaking to him again.

"Good day, Captain," Beatrice said, resting the book in her lap. "Did you enjoy your visit to the cathedral yesterday?"

Was he also going to be reprimanded for his conversation with her sister? The situation was going from bad to worse.

"Yes. It was quite informative. Your sister has an extraordinary gift of painting pictures with words. She made the Scottish invasion come alive. I understand why she is an acclaimed writer."

Lady Elkington beamed with pride.

He turned toward Alicia and saw the flush rise from her neck to her cheeks.

"You're most gracious, Captain." Alicia turned quickly away and faced her sister. "Beatrice, are you ready to leave?"

"You'll do anything to keep me from reading this story." Lady Elkington placed a lace ribbon in the book, closed it, and set it on the table.

Justin stifled a gasp. Neither of them realized who he was. He was sure Elkington had told them.

Go on. Get it over with. Say something. Now. At least you will leave with some dignity. He wasn't sure if Alicia would throw him out and at the moment, he didn't want to risk that.

He said nothing.

Coward.

"Yes. I'm ready." Lady Elkington stood and led the way to the foyer. "I'm eager to find a locket for Elkington."

The ladies donned their pelisses, pinned on their bonnets, and took their reticules. They filed out of the manor and into the Barrington carriage for the short ride to the top of the promontory and the castle.

The women chatted about the upcoming Harvest Party. They teased and tortured each other the same way he, his brother and their cousin did. Their affection for each other was obvious.

At the castle, Justin handed them down from the carriage. Alicia shook out her skirt.

"Alicia, you and the captain go along. I'll meet you at the tearoom. I shan't be long. I'll tell the modiste you chose the robin's egg blue for your new pelisse." Beatrice turned to him. "Take care. If you think my sister paints pretty pictures of the cathedral, wait until she tells you about the castle and its intrigues. Now, if you will forgive me. I'm off to the jeweler."

Lady Elkington didn't wait for a response, she hurried away toward one of the shops. He and Alicia continued to the castle gate.

"You're very quiet." He marveled at the determination marked on her face. "Are you planning a new story?"

"Forgive me, Captain. My sister has it in her head to give Elkington a gift and has decided on an engraved locket with a ringlet of her hair."

"You don't approve?" The woman continued to be a surprise. He was under the impression all women enjoyed tokens of affection.

"I don't approve of a peace offering. I advised her to speak with Elkington and discuss the issue and not to ignore it. A peace offering is no way to settle a difference of opinion. The delay only makes the issue worse. Don't you agree?"

"Yes. It takes courage to face difficult issues, especially ones that may be hurtful."

She was correct, of course. He couldn't avoid his difficult issue. He appreciated her sister's dilemma, but the woman had nothing to worry about. Elkington was mad for his wife.

If only he could be certain that Alicia was mad about him.

"You and I are in agreement. Elkington and my sister are a love match, but that does not prevent him from acting thick headed at times. And if you ask them what they are arguing about, both will say they have no idea. The truth is the issue is unimportant." She gasped. "I didn't mean to bore you with family issues."

"That proves you care deeply about both of them."

"I do and I want them to resolve the real issue. The rest of the world may not see her as a smart, thinking, and capable woman. But Elkington must or he'll destroy the very thing he loves about her."

Her insight astounded him. Not that she loved her sister or Elkington, that he expected. She was asking her sister to resolve the deeper underlying issue to strengthen their relationship.

⇒⇒⇒⇐⇐⇐

THEY CAME THROUGH the castle gate into the bailey. Alicia navigated them around a stone marker, *Margaret's Miracle*, and stopped where he could get a good view of the place. Like many buildings in a similar condition, the castle was in ruins. Scaffolding surrounded the keep, the recent repairs in various stages of completion.

"You'll see there are many small houses inside the bailey. At one time, all the villagers lived here. Like many old villages, the only way to assure safety was inside the castle walls. The old houses are being removed in order to restore the castle to its early glory."

Justin took a torch from the grate, and they entered the keep.

They climbed the narrow flight of steps. The hall widened at the top and led to a large archway. They entered and stood in the center of the great hall, ravaged by time and neglect. Visitors walked around the edges of the room examining the fallen stones and the few wall engravings that remained.

"I've been in castles on the Continent that are in the same condition. Some have been the inspiration for my stories. I find it a bit difficult to write as a former captain and adopted my mother's family name—"

"Sommer-by-the-Sea is filled with inspiration. While I don't use the actual names of locations here, those who live in the village enjoy identifying the places I reference. My heroine appears in all my stories."

"Why?" he asked.

She was caught off guard by his question, yet excited to provide him, a promising author, with direction and encouragement. "With each story the reader learns more about her and witnesses her growth. Do you have any recurring characters in your stories?"

"The villain. My readers learn about him. They witness his

descent into hell. He'll be in every story until I put an end to him. At the moment, I haven't figured that out."

All he needed was some inspiration to help him find his ending. *There are any number of places that would do.* But which one would be best? She said nothing for some time while she let her mind wander.

"Forgive me. I didn't mean to upset you," he said.

"Oh, you didn't upset me. I have something I want you to see. It's just the place to put your villain when you catch him. Follow me."

She led him back to the main level and down the staircase leading to the depths of the castle. They went along a passageway and entered a vaulted chamber filled with deteriorating columns the size of tree trunks. Two doors on either side of the room stood ajar. A light flickered in one and drew their attention.

"Come. You'll see what I mean." They entered the small cell and found a couple examining the prisoners' carvings on the wall. Justin put the torch on the wall bracket next to theirs.

Alicia stood back as Justin scanned the cell, his face a mixture of surprise and appreciation.

"This is how I imagined the dungeon after listening to your description," he said. "From the cobwebs to the broken manacles hanging from the wall, you left nothing out."

She felt her cheeks warm and gave him a deep nod, accepting his compliment.

"I enjoyed your story about the cathedral. You must have another about the castle," he said.

Alicia had just the tale to tell him.

"Months after the Scottish invasion, Sir Whitaker, you remember I told you he was the mayor."

"Yes. I remember. He transported the Scottish prisoners from this awful dungeon into the tower to protect the cathedral from being bombarded."

She smiled and nodded, pleased he paid attention to her history lesson.

"Every month, a Scottish trader's ship docked at our shore. The Highlander captain met the mayor's daughter and as it happens, the two developed a tendre for each other. Neither wanted to part, but he had to go back to Scotland. He promised her he'd return."

Alicia nodded to the other couple who had moved closer and gave her their attention.

"His word proved to be good. Each month, he sailed into Sommer-by-the-Sea and spent time with his sweetheart. At night with the town gate locked tight, she longed to see her Highlander. She would steal into the abandoned castle dungeons and slip out through a little-known tunnel and meet him on the beach."

The woman moved closer to her escort, a hopeful expression on her face. Alicia was encouraged to go on.

"They spent their time together talking and watching the sun rise, possibly stealing a kiss or two before she returned to her room.

"When her father found out about their rendezvous, he went into a tirade. The next time the ship was spotted coming into port, the mayor confronted his daughter outside the keep. He stopped her and accused her of seeing the brigand. She stood in front of everyone and declared her love for her Highlander."

The woman gasped, her fingers at her lips. The gentleman put his arm around her for comfort.

"Furious, the mayor dragged his daughter from the spot and locked her in the castle dungeon. He confronted the Highlander and told him he had taken his daughter to a place where he would never find her and forbid him to set foot in Sommer-by-the-Sea again upon pain of death."

"Oh, no," the woman whispered. Then, she said, "I'm so sorry. I didn't mean to interrupt. Please go on."

"Yes, please do," the woman's escort said.

Alicia nodded then turned to Justin. "The Highlander cursed her father and boiled with anger that the mayor had treated his love so badly. He returned to his ship.

"The villagers were abuzz with how the mayor treated his

daughter, but the last time anyone saw the girl, was when she was dragged into the keep. No one knew where he had taken her.

"Meanwhile, the Highlander's first mate, a likeable man, had been in the village tavern and found where the woman was being held. Within the hour, the Highlander sailed out of the port. The mayor watched from his window, content he had solved his problem.

"But the mayor was angry with his daughter. To teach her a lesson, he left her in the dark, dank dungeon all night. She would realize just how much compassion and honor her Highlander had for her. How could anyone who loved someone let her suffer all night?"

The woman looked around at the cramped cell. The gentleman tenderly pulled her closer.

"The following day, pleased with himself, the mayor planned to shower his daughter with attention, for he loved her dearly. He entered the castle and with a torch in hand descended to the dungeon, took the key from the holder on the wall, and unlocked the door. When he entered the cell, he was startled to find it empty. He searched everywhere but did not find her. He hurried home, angry she had fooled him, but he didn't find her there either. He waited days, weeks, months but she didn't return. He spent the rest of his life trying to untangle the puzzle."

"Is there more to this story?" the other woman said.

"The miracle is no one has the answer to the puzzle. Perhaps the captain has a suggestion?"

The woman, her companion, and Alicia waited for Justin's answer.

"The Highlander called his clan to his side." He turned to Alicia. "He was heartbroken without his love. He returned with his warriors."

Alicia nodded. Encouraged, he continued.

"In the dead of night, they entered the mayor's house. They fought. Even though wounded, no one was able to stop the Highlander. After searching everywhere, he at last cornered the mayor, his sword at his throat. Before he made his demand, the mayor swore to him he had no knowledge of what happened to his daughter. The man asked the Highlander to kill him because he would die a little each day not knowing what had become of her. The Highlander did not give the mayor the relief he sought. He left, leaving the mayor a broken man. The mayor lived the rest of his days never seeing his daughter again."

He was quiet when he was done. Alicia touched his arm, a worried expression on her face.

"Well done, Captain. Thank you for the lovely story."

The woman and her companion left, leaving them alone.

"As you said, the Highlander made sure the mayor suffered," Alicia's voice held a note of approval. "But there is more. After confronting the mayor, the Highlander left the harbor. Out at sea, he and his love stood on his ship as they sailed into Edinburgh."

"He knew where the little-known tunnel was located." Justin's voice rose with renewed energy and excitement. "And the mayor left the key in sight."

"Yes. When the Highlander came to her, he wrapped her in his plaid and told her, 'My heart is yours forever and always.'"

When he spoke again, his voice was soft and tender. "What was her response?"

The silver streaks in his eyes flashed with warmth and passion. For the moment he was the only thing in the world that mattered. She lowered her gaze, afraid he would see feelings she wasn't prepared to admit.

"As mine…" She took a breath, surprised by the tingling in the pit of her stomach. "Is yours."

"*Margaret's Miracle*. The Highlander's sweetheart was Margaret," he whispered as he stepped closer. "But didn't her father know about the tunnel?"

"The tunnel was not a secret to the villagers." Alicia hoped he would move closer. "You Highlanders are a crafty lot. After they escaped, her love had the tunnel closed with rocks as if it had caved in. When the mayor found the cell empty, he ran to the tunnel. He was sure his daughter had used it for her escape. But when he got to its entrance, he stood dumbfounded to find it had collapsed. The mayor wasn't able to explain her disappearance. He never saw her again. He spent his life ruing the day he treated her so badly."

Alicia raised her chin, her lips trembling and tears running down her cheek. "She gave up everything for her Highlander."

He pulled her into his arms, holding her close.

She closed her eyes and reveled in his warmth and tenderness, then slid her arms around him. The touch of his hand at her cheek was almost unbearable in its tenderness.

A deep breath had her content and smiling at the scent of lavender and citrus, his scent.

"Did she regret her decision?" he murmured softly into her hair.

"No. Why would she regret finding her true love? She stood by him and made him proud she would be his wife. They were able to do anything, as long as they did it together."

She lifted her chin and stared into his eyes.

They stood that way for several moments, neither of them moving, neither of them willing to break the spell.

HER EYES WERE beautiful, expressive, and filled with passion. He brushed a tender kiss across her forehead. He wasn't sure who he consoled, her or himself.

"It's a tender story. You tell it well." His voice was low and mellow.

"I'm afraid I dampened your coat." She looked down and wiped his lapel. Her hand stroked his chest.

It was a small torture, but torture, nonetheless. She remained tucked next to him. He took advantage and brought her closer. She didn't resist.

"No matter." His voice was a whisper.

Even though they had only recently met, each time he was

with her the pull became stronger. He had never wanted anyone as he wanted her.

He was breathing hard, and his heart was pounding. It took all his strength not to crush her to him and kiss her cheeks, lips, neck…everywhere.

He didn't want the moment to end, but he needed to be sensible. They were alone and knew it was unwise to take such liberties.

"We best return to your sister."

She nodded without saying a word.

He reluctantly released her, retrieved the torch, and helped her up the stairs. After he returned the torch, she took his offered arm, and they made their way out the castle gate.

"I enjoyed your stories. Each was about devotion, the first, devotion to country, the second, devotion to each other. The stories seem to come easily to you."

"Whenever Beatrice got in trouble, which wasn't very often, she'd ask me for a solution. Creative writing was my best subject."

"Why, Lady Alicia, you surprise me." He put his hand over his heart, feigning surprise, and let out a hearty laugh.

"If you tell anyone I will deny it," she whispered.

"I assure you that your secret is safe with me." His optimism soared as they continued toward the tearoom.

"I hope you enjoyed today's excursion," she said.

"Thoroughly. The company and the stories. Collaborating with you on a new ending for *Margaret's Miracle* was… invigorating."

Anonymous' words were not lost on him.

"Imagine if these authors combined their skills? They would lay out a plot with characters to keep you reading until the last page or until your candle burns out."

Was it possible the reviewer was more perceptive than he

first thought? This exercise had him thinking.

They entered the tearoom and spotted Beatrice. Alicia led the way to the table.

"Stories swirl around in my head. They were based on some piece of information. I've told you two. The first one was based on facts and is well documented. The other is a folk tale." She leaned toward him. "No one can answer why the stone is engraved or what *Margaret's Miracle* references."

He helped her into the chair next to her sister and took his seat across from her.

"The tale grew out of a need to explain the stone," Alicia added as she settled in her seat.

"What stories?" Beatrice asked as she poured tea and handed him his cup.

"Lady Alicia told me about *Margaret's Miracle*. Do you think it's a true story or a folk tale?" he asked and sipped his tea. His heart had returned to its normal beat, but he couldn't take his eyes off of Alicia.

"Many stories exist explaining the stone. They range from Margaret being denounced a witch for having predicted an eclipse, to the humiliation of birthing a child out of wedlock and insisting she was still pure. Each had a wretched ending. With those choices, I prefer to believe my sister's version of a love story."

"The captain and I developed a new ending. True love conquers all. Was your visit to the jeweler a success?" Alicia asked.

Beatrice pursed her lips and gave a half-hearted shrug.

"I didn't see anything that I..." Beatrice took Alicia's hand and gave it a squeeze. "No. I thought about our discussion and decided to put off the gift."

Justin witnessed the shared silent moment between the sisters and Alicia's grace in accepting the compliment without comment.

"You won't be sorry."

Beatrice turned toward him. "Tell me, Captain, have you seen enough of Sommer-by-the-Sea?"

"Have I, Lady Alicia?" He looked at her over the rim of his teacup.

"Not at all. You haven't been to the beach. No visit to Sommer-by-the-Sea is complete without experiencing it."

"In this weather? Your villagers must be a hearty bunch." He tried not to smile and wondered if she swam. If she did, he would take her to his home in Scotland to the lake where they could spend the day swimming and…He felt a rush of heat and pushed his thoughts aside.

"Not for bathing. The beach is a wonderful place to walk and get lost in your thoughts. I do some of my best thinking walking along the rocks and sand."

"Very well. I look forward to the expedition when I return." He put his cup down.

"I must have misunderstood," Alicia muttered hastily. "I thought you were staying for several weeks."

He was caught off guard by the disappointment in her voice.

"You're not mistaken. I leave for Edinburgh this evening. A family obligation."

Alicia nodded without saying anything.

"I return Monday. The ship docks at the break of dawn."

Her face brightened and his spirits soared.

"Then we're all settled. Monday late morning," Alicia said, the usual brightness back in her voice.

"Captain, you must try the biscuits. Alicia's friend Lady Euphemia says they are the best in all England."

Justin sampled the confection. Alicia's friend *was* a good judge of biscuits, but then, anything would taste good at the moment.

Tea over, he handed them up to the carriage. The ride to Hartmore Manor was filled with chatter. He didn't say much. Instead, he enjoyed the pleasant company.

Their ride ended much too soon for his liking. He thanked them both for an enjoyable afternoon. Upon his return to Sommer Chase, he entered the house with a light step and of all things, whistling.

CHAPTER SEVEN

J USTIN BOARDED THE *Sommer Wind* and sailed out of the harbor
at ten on the evening's high tide. It was a full day's sail to
Edinburgh if the winds and weather held.

He looked forward to being with Lawson. The last time they
were together, they spent the night drinking and telling stories,
each one more daring than the last. He could almost taste the ale
and hear the man's hearty laugh.

He settled in his cabin for a long night. With a tankard of ale
and lit lantern hanging from the beam, he opened his portmanteau to ready himself for bed. Wedged on the side underneath his
extra shirt he found the copy of *The Lost Dowry*. He had tossed it
in his luggage during the coach ride to Sommer-by-the-Sea.

Alicia's stories enchanted him. The passion in her telling the
folk tale carried him along. The story was enjoyable, but not as
much as working together to cobble the new ending.

He examined the cover. Was her full-length story as good as
her impromptu ones? He settled on the bunk and opened her
book. He read the first page, the next, and the next. Her writing
held him captive from the start.

He applauded her heroine Clarissa through one tragedy after
another.

With a sizeable dowry and an acceptable but loveless marriage, Clarissa's intended left her waiting at the altar. The bride-

groom escaped to places unknown to avoid being pressed into military service. Justin's anger built. He could not abide with such a person.

He might not have taken Clarissa with him, but he did take her dowry. Her reputation was in ruins, the family fortune lost. Gossip ran rampant, but no one was willing to come to her aid. Clarissa needed to retrieve her dowry to save the family.

Justin's mind went wild with strategies and plans, from where she should look to what she should do.

Finally, an acquaintance of her father's offered assistance. But Justin's relief was short-lived. He bristled at the villain who proclaimed he loved her but used her badly.

Her pride and self-esteem took another blow when she found his intentions were to take the money for himself.

He cheered Clarissa's resourcefulness when she and her maid set out on a series of adventures to retrieve her funds, and she was able to turn her situation around and emerge courageous and strong.

The cabin brightened as the sun rose sending a ray of light through the port hole. He turned down the lantern's wick. Tired as he was, he kept reading until the last word. The book closed and laying on his chest, he was unwilling to move for fear he'd break the story's magic.

How did she make him care about this fictitious character? He rose and tucked the book into his luggage, regretting the story was over. He wanted more.

Dressed and with gear in hand, he went onto the deck. The cool North Sea air refreshed him. His hands clasped and his elbows on the rail, he watched the sun brighten and began to understand her writing strategy.

The essence of her story was a woman fighting against obstacles and willing to sacrifice her own happiness in order to hold her family together. The depth of the heroine's character impressed him. Clarissa was competent, had her flaws, as well as a noble cause, and was inventive and clever in finding solutions.

She grabbed or created opportunities where she could.

At every turn she learned and grew into a new version of herself. Her challenges were easily understandable. The admiration he held for this fictional woman astounded him. Clarissa didn't exist, yet he felt he knew her.

A splash of sea spray startled him and brought him back to the present.

Did his writing stir similar feelings?

Her story was a romance. Clarissa and… He straightened, startled by the thought that flashed in his mind. He'd found the story's flaw. He couldn't remember the hero's name or note the actions he had taken to support Clarissa's cause. The hero was a weak secondary character. Developing a worthy romantic interest would have made this story perfect.

He took the book from his luggage and skimmed through the story looking for places where her hero could step forward and support Clarissa in her quest – where the hero would be more meaningful.

He was eager to return to Sommer-by-the-Sea and speak with Alicia. But would she accept his suggestions? Would she even listen to him once he told her his pen name? Disheartened, he put her book back in his bag. Would she remain with Caulfield Publishing?

He gazed at the sea as the schooner glided along and for a moment wished it could swallow him up rather than have to face Alicia. It was a ridiculous idea, but he dreaded her disappointment and, if he were honest, the possibility she would never speak to him again.

The activity on the deck increased as the ship entered the Forth and made its way to Leith.

Justin checked his watch. Lawson would be waiting for him at the White Hart Inn. The small, intimate inn on the Grassmarket was his cousin's favorite. Sitting in the far corner with his tankard of ale, he had a full view of the room and everyone in it.

Forty minutes later, he walked into the inn. Lawson, at his

favorite table, signaled him to join him.

"Lass, bring another tankard," Lawson said to the barmaid.

The woman had the ale on the table before Justin could put down his portmanteau. For a moment, he stood in front of his cousin.

"Are you well?" Justin's brow wrinkled with a concerned look.

"Why do you ask?" Lawson glared at him.

"One tankard? The last time I was here, the table was filled with your empty tankards."

Lawson's glare turned into a loud laugh. "I don't want you to feel bad. I had them taken away, so we can start over again."

Justin took a seat and a pull of the ale. The lass came by again and put bannocks and cheese on the table.

"You're looking better than the last time we spoke, lad. While you've been gone, I've kept an eye on Mrs. Lewis and her boy, Eli. They are doing fine. I found her employment as you asked. She was working for a merchant in his dry goods store."

"Was? Has she moved on?" If Lawson couldn't find her a position, perhaps he should speak to Miller.

Lawson enjoyed drawing out his stories. He fancied himself a good storyteller. Justin would have to be patient. There was no moving him any faster than he wanted to go.

"She has indeed. She married the man," Lawson said. "He gave his business here to his brother to manage and moved his new wife and son to Glasgow."

"You're a matchmaker as well. I'll keep that in mind." Justin had more ale. "I'm glad she and the boy are settled." He looked about at the crowd of people.

"Where are Sean and the others?'

"I wanted some time with you alone. Not to worry. They will not miss a chance to drink you under the table."

Lawson and his men made many attempts to out-drink him. It continued to be a source of amusement since he was a young lad.

His cousin moved closer and leaned toward him.

"I don't know how much Barrington told you and, for your own good, I will not tell you more than is needed. I've confirmed that the problem in Sommer-by-the-Sea is more than free traders and smuggling. Treachery is afoot. This lot is vile. They'd as soon cut your throat than tip their hat to you. Everyone's lips are sealed shut. I cannot find more than a breath of information."

"Barrington mentioned accurate information was difficult to find." Justin changed to a business focus.

"Aye. I cannot go to him without causing suspicion. Nor have him or anyone else come here. You were the one person who has been here often and would not raise any suspicion."

His cousin wasn't an overly cautious man. He was willing to allow events to occur without worrying what happened afterwards. This cautious attitude made Justin stop and think that the situation was more serious than Barrington led him to believe.

"Visiting you is not a hardship." He took a long drag of the ale.

Lawson nodded, raised his tankard, and took a pull.

Justin raised his ale and inhaled the nostalgic scent, different than the English varieties.

"Foreigners are involved. I don't pay much attention since there are always people from other places muddying the water." His cousin's gaze was fixed on him. "That was, until *your* name was mentioned."

Justin paused his tankard raised halfway to his mouth. "The only people interested in me are the French, and a particular French person at that." His stomach clenched at the thought of the man.

Lawson took another gulp and finished his ale.

Justin looked at the table and concentrated on the voices around him, listening for a particular one and the man's signature phrase, *qui vivra verra:* wait and see.

Nothing. He let out a deep breath. He resisted rubbing the

scars on his chest. They had faded into silvery jagged lines and did what the Frenchman intended.

Remind him of their time together.

"It's a rumor. None of us have it from the foreigner's mouth. We wouldn't know him if he stood in front of us. Like you, none of us have ever seen him. I was told he said his new adventure will be in your next book."

"The Frenchman is with Napoleon in Elba. Besides, anyone can claim they are my villain." Justin raised his head and let out a deep breath. "Even in my stories, the villain keeps his face covered when he tortures, excuse me, *interrogates* captives. He taunts them, telling them they will never know if he is the man behind them at the tobacconist, or on the dancefloor with their wife."

"But you're not afraid of shadows. You're a Melrose and made of stronger stuff. His little parlor game cannot stop you." Lawson signaled for another round.

The Frenchman was one reason Justin spoke to the families of survivors. Not only for them, but for himself. Each visit reminded him why he needed to find the Frenchman and put an end to that ghost once and for all.

"Will that be all, sir?" the barmaid asked.

"For now, lass," Lawson said and waited until she was gone.

"After I put the few snips of information together, I found them worrisome. *If* the foreigner is your Frenchman who does Napoleon's bidding, what is he doing in England? And why is he smuggling brandy?" He raised the fresh tankard in salute.

"He is a high-ranking officer and part of Napoleon's inner circle. He wouldn't be here. Napoleon wouldn't let him out of his sight."

"There's more. Colonel Campbell, Napoleon's chaperone in Elba leaves for England on Wednesday. That's when Napoleon wants his henchman *back* in Elba."

"I cannot imagine the Frenchman a free trader and smuggling brandy," Justin said.

"I agree. That's one of the things I find worrisome." Lawson put his tankard down. "You're not going to let that cheese and good bannock go to waste, are you?"

Justin pushed the plate toward him.

"So, the puzzle is why is the Frenchman here. I'm sure Barrington will be interested." Justin finished his ale and signaled the barmaid.

Sean and Liam came through the door and made their way toward them.

"You mentioned this is one of the things you found worrisome. Is there more?" Justin asked.

"Not really worrisome. It's a personal issue. I need your help winning a wager."

"I'm listening." Justin sipped his ale. Lawson was not one to ask him for help.

"I need a battle strategy."

Justin almost spit out his ale.

Sean pounded him on the back.

"I told him I would write it for him," Sean said.

"You can't write," Justin said to Sean, and turned to his cousin. "What have you gotten yourself into?"

Lawson scratched his head and gave him a sheepish glance.

"I may have given the impression that I could write a good battle strategy. Like you."

Justin threw back his head and burst out laughing.

"What's so funny? This is a life-or-death issue. There's gold at stake." Lawson glared at him.

"It would serve you right if I left right now."

"You'd have my blood, the blood of your own clansman on your hands." Lawson gave a quick nod and sat back. A fresh tankard of ale was set in front of him.

Justin finished his ale.

"The name of the clan would be ruined."

"Oh, in that case I'll have to help you." Justin picked up his cousin's tankard and downed it all at once. "Tell me about this bet."

"That's a good lad," Lawson said, rubbing his hands together, calling to the barmaid. "Lass, four more."

"Now for the serious drinking."

MRS. BAINBRIDGE'S SALON was abuzz with Alicia and the others.

"I spotted you at the castle yesterday. Pat and I were on our way to speak with you when your sister grabbed us," Effie said.

"By the time she left, you and the handsome gentleman were going through the castle gate," Pat said. "Who is he?"

Alicia smiled to herself. She could kiss Beatrice. If Pat and Effie had come up to her and Captain Caulfield, there would be no getting rid of them.

"Gentleman? Oh, you must mean my publisher's nephew, Captain Caulfield."

"Captain? Alicia, we saw you laughing and taking his arm," Effie said. "Beatrice conveniently prevented us from speaking to you."

"Why is your publisher's nephew here?" Pat asked.

Alicia gave them a wide smile. There was no fooling her friends.

"He served with Lord Barrington and is visiting him. Since he was going to Sommer-by-the-Sea, his uncle asked him to deliver the books for the reading next week. Please, I'm simply entertaining my publisher's nephew."

"That's a relief. I thought he was, well my thoughts are not important. When will you introduce me to him?" Pat said, looking at Alicia over her cup of tea.

Alicia felt her face blanch and had nothing to say.

Pat put her cup down and gave her a wicked smirk. "Just as I thought. He is someone special. Alicia Hartley, you must tell us who he is."

Alicia glared at Pat with a stare that would turn anyone into stone.

"That won't work on me. I was the one who taught you that particular stare." Pat got up from her seat and moved to Alicia's side.

Alicia straightened out her skirt and smiled. "I literally walked into him at my publisher's office," she said.

"What happened next?" Effie asked.

Everyone gave Alicia their full attention.

AIDED BY HIGHER than usual winds and tides, the *Sommer Wind* docked at six on Monday morning. Tired, but eager to leave his report for Barrington and the others, Justin hurried to Sommer Chase. Lawson was good at ferreting out information and what he gave Justin wouldn't disappoint Barrington and the others.

At half-nine, he entered the breakfast room. Sun streamed through the windows. It was a welcome change from the stormy night. He was looking forward to his jaunt on the beach with Alicia and was relieved the weather cooperated.

"Good morning." Barrington, Peter, Simon and Nicolas were still at breakfast. He took a plate from the sideboard and helped himself to toasted bread with jam, eggs and bacon.

"James still hasn't arrived?" he asked.

"No. He hasn't returned from Kent. He should be here in another day or two," Barrington said, buttering his toast.

Justin took a seat next to Nicholas. He nodded at Giles, Barrington's footman, to pour him coffee.

"Thank you for your report. We read it this morning. Your information confirms what we've found."

"This is much more than a simple smuggling enterprise," Nicolas said.

"I'm well aware," Justin said. "With the Frenchman involved, this is not a task that the Land Guard can handle by themselves. From what Lawson said, these men are vicious and will not be deterred."

"The Sea and Land Guard spend most of their time and energy close to London. That leaves the forces thin here. Which makes Sommer-by-the-Sea a good place for this operation," Peter said.

"I agree." Barrington managed a bit more jam on his toast.

"If this is the work of the Frenchman, we can expect well calculated plans, the type for which he's known." Justin sat poised with the fork in his hand.

"Sommer-by-the-Sea is far from any military encampment," Barrington said. "The locals are aware of some activity and attribute it to a simple smuggling venture."

"Some may be naïve and give them support and others may ignore them, afraid to get involved." Justin ate his eggs.

"The people here are not easily fooled," Barrington said, finishing his coffee. "But, as you well know, the Frenchman has a way of manipulating people to his will."

Justin nodded and continued eating.

"I know you're right." Barrington wiped his mouth with his serviette. "I don't like this. Whatever the plan, it must be executed by Wednesday in order for the Frenchman to return to Elba."

"No, I don't like this at all." Barrington threw his serviette to the table. "We can't protect all of Sommer-by-the-Sea. And we have no idea who we can trust."

"I'll speak to Commander Russell in Bamburgh. We have enough information to arouse his attention. I'll leave right away." Peter rose from the table.

"I'll go with you. Russell and I served together," Simon said.

Barrington nodded.

"The closest Land Guard post is in Harrogate." Nicolas stood eating the last of his biscuit. "They may be able to speak to their superiors and provide us with some help."

The three men left.

"What are your plans?" Barrington asked Justin.

"Lady Alicia is taking me to the beach. She mentioned caves. If they're anything like the caves in Spain, they may make a good place to stow contraband. I'll scout the area for any signs of activity."

"Lady Alicia. She is a lovely woman. I'm not surprised you have an affinity for her, the two of you being authors. A bit headstrong, and I'm sure you realize she is not one to conform with convention. She is one of Honoria's favorite graduates." Barrington chuckled.

"Honoria? Have I met her?"

A flush rushed up Barrington's neck. "Mrs. Bainbridge is the mistress of the female seminary. Her late husband and I were at Eton together."

Justin nodded. There was more there than Barrington was going to admit, but that was a story for another day.

"Enjoy your morning. If Elkington has returned from London, give him the details of your report and ask him to join us."

Justin left Barrington and prepared for his morning with Alicia. As he left Sommer Chase for Hartmore Manor, he hoped with all his heart that Elkington had not yet returned.

CHAPTER EIGHT

JUSTIN SPENT THE twenty-minute walk along the river to Hartmore Manor crafting what to say to Elkington. He did not care about the information about the smugglers. Barrington had put that into a letter. No, he was more concerned about how to explain his inability to reveal his pen name to Alicia: that had turned into a dilemma.

The closer he got to the hall, the more he prepared for the verbal lashing he deserved. By the time he arrived in front of the house he was prepared for battle.

He came through the gate and caught sight of a movement in the drawing room window. He went to the door and tugged on the bell pull.

"Good morning, Captain Caulfield. Lady Alicia is expecting you. This way please."

The butler ushered him into the drawing room.

"Good morning, Lady Alicia." He stepped into the room, his face brightening at the sight of her.

Alicia turned toward him from settling the curtains in place.

"Good morning, Captain Caulfield." The voice came from behind him.

He turned abruptly and faced Lady Elkington, who tried to hide her faint amusement.

"Lady Elkington." He nodded with a gracious smile. "Will

Captain Elkington be joining us?" His jaw muscles tightened, but he succeeded in keeping his smile pleasant.

"I regret my husband has not returned from London," she said.

He didn't know if he was relieved or terrified. This was only a reprieve, but not for long. He had to tell her before tomorrow's reading.

"The weather has cleared nicely for our adventure. There is a more direct way to reach the beach. Rather than a carriage ride along the river, we'll walk across the heath. That route provides a different vantage point of the village."

"As you wish."

"The weather is unusually warm for November and last night's wind has turned into a breeze. It should be an invigorating, pleasant walk."

"I'm glad you're pleased. Shall we?" He motioned to the door. The ladies gracefully swept past him.

They strolled through the heath. The breeze sent ripples along the uncultivated landscape on the top of the cliff filled with its purple and pink heather as well as wild bilberry bushes.

"I'm surprised no one else is here. Last month, the area was filled with people picking berries and gathering honey for the yearly Harvest Festival."

"Sane people are all warm and cozy baking their pies and cakes or brewing their wine and beer for the festival contest," Lady Elkington said then turned to Justin. "Our village is well-known for bilberries – *blaeberries* – and the nectar from the heather produces some of the finest honey."

"The awards will be given out at Mrs. Miller's Harvest Salon," Alicia said.

"Will you be competing?" he asked although he didn't think either Alicia or her sister were inclined to bake or brew.

"My sister will not easily admit it, but she is the current champion. Beatrice makes a very unique tart filled with bilberries and apples. No one can pry the recipe from her. She has the kitchen staff sworn to secrecy."

"Captain, don't believe her. I am more than happy to share my recipe, for the right price."

That set the three of them chuckling. They continued until they reached the cliffs and took in the sea.

"Isn't it a magnificent view? I could stand here all day watching the water and the clouds. I don't think I will ever tire of it." Alicia turned to him. "Ready for our adventure?"

"By all means." He gave one arm to Lady Alicia and his other to her sister.

"I enjoy walking along the beach during low tide," Alicia said as they made their way down the path and onto the packed sand.

"Up ahead, past the sharp bend on the beach we'll see caves. Several are submerged during high tide, but accessible when the tide is out."

He stared at the cliff and made out several caves midway up the face. Those would be difficult to access. They walked further down the beach and passed a bend. Two caves came into view.

These were located at the foot of the wall. He studied the cliff face searching for the watermark and found it yards above the entrances. These must be the caves Alicia referenced that filled when the tide was in.

He glanced toward the sea. At low tide the beach extended for some distance. Ships could not approach. He looked back at the cave. Nor would it be easy to see from a great distance especially in the late afternoon. The sun set at roughly four in the afternoon. It would be completely dark by low tide an hour later.

"It couldn't be safe to go inside," he murmured more to himself.

"That was my adventure, my challenge, to stay in the cave as long as possible," Alicia said.

He spun around and faced her. The innocent expression on her face did not move him.

"It was Alicia's adventure, not mine," Lady Elkington said. "Our parents forbid us to go near the caves."

"And rightly so," he said with an authoritative air.

"They were not pleased we walked on the beach, either. Alicia enjoyed flirting with the surf, daring it to capture her. I cannot count how many times she tried to sneak into the house with the hem of her skirts soaking wet."

He looked at the entrance. Smugglers could stow their plunder at the evening low tide. No one would be the wiser. Even if the Sea Guard searched the shoreline with a spyglass, the ships would be far from shore.

"I always loved coming to the beach. The spray carried on the wind and the waves, the way they crash and swirl." Alicia looked into his eyes. "Don't you think they're beautiful?"

"Yes, Lady Alicia." His voice was low and soft. The cave and Barrington's issue forgotten. He didn't see the turbulent ocean. He was too busy dealing with a different tempest.

"Quite beautiful."

Her eyes widened before she turned from him and walked toward the cave, but not before he observed the deep flush creeping from her neck toward her cheek.

"Are you coming, Beatrice?" she asked.

"I have no interest in traipsing up that slick rock to peer into a smelly cave. I didn't do it when we were girls. I don't like that place. I'll wait here." Her sister didn't budge. "Be careful, Captain. The water and waves have polished the rocks. You'll find it difficult to keep your footing."

They left Lady Elkington standing on the beach while he and Alicia continued on into the cave.

The moderate grotto reeked of seaweed and brine. Rocks, large boulders along with frayed rope, driftwood, lengths of old chain, and broken crates littered the floor.

He evaluated the area as if it were a military objective. The right side of the floor sloped up. Rocks and large boulders smoothed by the water created a maze. The cave continued, but without a torch he didn't want to venture further than the natural light allowed.

It didn't take much imagination to see that the place was perfect for smugglers.

He followed Alicia as she made her way among the boulders that towered over their head.

"How do you find your way in here without getting turned around?" he asked after several twists and turns.

She took his hand and rubbed it against the stone.

"Do you feel the marks?"

The suddenness and intimacy of her action startled him. Her hand was warm and soft. She was an intoxicating creature who had no knowledge of the effect she had on him.

With great difficulty, he pulled his mind away from her warm hand and imagining how other parts of her would be soft and concentrated on the stone under his fingers.

"An arrow?" He traced the marking with his finger and looked to his right. "Pointing in that direction?"

"Yes." Her eyes sparkled. "I thought I was so clever. However, Father was not happy with me when I came in one afternoon, dropped a chisel and gouged his desk."

"You made these marks with only a chisel?"

"No, of course not. I used a stone to pound on the tool. It was quite effective. But the cave did teach me a lesson. I thought I was going to die."

Die? What was the threat? On alert, he instinctively stepped closer to her ready to take action.

She turned to the sloping side of the cave. "Beatrice and I were playing on the beach. It was my turn to hide from her. She hid behind the large rocks on the beach. I came in here. If Beatrice did venture in, she would never go deep into the cave. I thought I was so clever."

He didn't have a good feeling about this.

"I went as far back as I dared, to the edge of the blackness."

A chill brushed across his shoulders. He breathed deeply to quell his building unease.

"There was a boulder high on the slope. It was the perfect

place to hide. The water would never come up that high."

He let out a low groan imagining what happened.

"I sat behind the boulder and waited. I heard Beatrice calling my name, walking all over the beach. As I thought, she didn't come inside the cave, and I didn't answer when she came to the entrance. If she found me, I knew she would tell Father where I hid. Eventually she went away."

"And you came out of your hiding place."

"Not right away. I laid my head against the boulder and waited a little longer. I listened to the rhythmic waves. It was hypnotic."

"You fell asleep?" he asked in a wave of panic. He tamped his fear down when he realized Lady Alicia was reliving hers.

"I woke when the water soaked my feet and skirts. In a fright, I made my way down the slope. When I reached the cave floor, the water was up to my knees and rushing in. I had to wade in waist deep water to get to the entrance escape. Wave after wave broke on the shore. The boulders on the beach were under water. Without seeing them, I had no way to navigate to the cliff path. But I couldn't stay where I was."

She looked up at him, her breath coming in spurts, her chest heaving. "I had no choice. I set out as best I could, trying to remember where the boulders were. Each wave forced me closer to the cliff wall. Several knocked me down and tugged me away toward the sea. All I could do was get up and try again until finally, I found the path."

As cool as it was, beads of sweat were on her forehead. Her eyes darted around wildly, looking for an escape route.

"Drenched and exhausted. I stood at the top of the cliff, my legs shaking. Father found me on my way home. I tried to make nothing of my condition. I told him I was caught by a wave. He looked so concerned. I couldn't tell him the truth and hated myself for it.

"As we made our way home, I told him I was laying on the large, flat rocks on the beach and didn't realize the tide was coming in. He scolded me good and proper. That was the first time I ever heard Father curse. *'You're bloody lucky you didn't get yourself killed.'* Before we reached home, I told him everything, especially how afraid I was. I think he was more afraid than I."

"Did that stop you from going into the caves?" he asked.

She was quiet and let out a sigh.

"I've been to the beach often, but this is the first time I've been inside the cave since the incident."

Neither of them said a word. For several moments all they heard was the crash of the waves outside the cave.

"My mother called me rambunctious," he said. "My father called me a growing boy. I stole cakes from the kitchen, swam in the lake with my friends, and played a warrior who conquered haystacks. I was the youngest in the group, but the biggest and also the target. While I could fight, I didn't."

"I wish I had known you when you were a boy. Imagine the adventures we would have had."

For a moment he was surrounded by an air of innocence tempered with strength and confidence. It was an idyllic time when he was a boy. What did he know of intrigue and war? It was a game. You pretended to kill your best friend and when it was all over, you both walked down the lane laughing, ready to do it all over again the next day.

He glanced at her and smiled. *She* wouldn't play the lady in distress, no, not Lady Alicia. Not a squire either. She would be a warrior, a Scottish warrior woman standing beside him and not expect any special consideration. He indeed could imagine the adventures they would have had.

"You never fought?" she asked, her tone suggested she didn't believe it.

"Finn, one of the boys, kept goading me. It was one insult after another. My father had warned me that I would be picked on because of my size and taught me I was a Highland warrior's son and had nothing to prove."

"You withstood his abuse. I am sure that was not easy."

"Everyone has their breaking point. I found mine when he pushed me into the well. Finn and his friends thought it was funny. At times I still hear his laugh echoing in the well as he closed the lid and left." He gave a nervous chuckle.

"How awful. He came back and got you out, sent down a rope, or sent someone to help you."

Justin's eyes had a faraway look. He was back in the well.

"How I screamed, but no one came. I spent the night in the dark on a narrow ledge cold and alone. The following morning my older cousin Matthew came to draw water for the horses. He fished me out without saying a word. I was cold through and through. He wrapped me in a blanket. On the way home, I told him everything. He stood with me and told my father what had been happening. My father went into a rage."

"What did he do?"

"We were at the mill several days later. Father was inside with the miller. Matthew stood at the door talking to the miller's daughter. I waited in the yard not too far away when Finn and his friends arrived. He started with his name calling. I ignored him. Matthew got my attention. I'll never forget his words. *Finish the little bastard so we can go home.* That's the version I can tell in your company."

"Did you?" She laughed.

"The first punch had him on his back. I lifted him and threw him into the horse trough. I turned to his friends and asked who was next. They ran down the lane.

"Father, Matthew and I went home singing. But the incident had a lasting effect. I'm still not fond of closed spaces, but when I went to war, I came face-to-face with my fear. I had no choice but to overcome it. On one campaign in Spain, I had to navigate a small cave, smaller than this one. Two of my men were held captive and I had to rescue them. There are still times when I am apprehensive."

"I can't imagine anything preventing you from taking action. How did you overcome your fear?" she asked.

"My men are loyal to me and I to them. I didn't have a choice. I put one foot in front of the other. My men had no doubt I would come for them or die trying. It was never a question. They would do the same for me. I would not allow the terror stabbing my heart or the icy panic to take control."

"I was right. Your loyalty and determination were stronger than your fear. It is commendable. Not everyone holds their values so dear."

He gazed at her in a new light. The woman was insightful, her thoughts deep and heartfelt.

"You are brave. At first, I found it too difficult to return to the beach, yet I was unhappy. I went to the cliff and stared at the rocks and sand but wasn't able to go down the path. My father gave me a solution."

She showed him her pendant. "I rub the amber. He called it a worry stone."

She let out a slight chuckle.

"The stone is a simple device that helps me quiet my mind and look at the true nature of a situation. It helps me calm my fears so I can move forward. In this case, return to the beach, walk in the surf, but examining my feelings about the cave was a different matter."

They stood in the cave quietly for several moments.

"I find it strange. I wanted you to see this place." She looked at him. "I had no doubt nothing would happen to me if you were with me."

She put her hand on his arm.

Surprised by the innocent gesture, he gave her a smile in return.

"Bringing you here seemed so right."

He lifted her hand to his lips and kissed it lightly.

She gasped but made no attempt to pull away from him.

He leaned down close, close enough for his cheeks to be bathed in her warm breath. He drove on and gently kissed her mouth.

Alicia didn't resist. Her lips were softer than he had imagined, and sweeter. His heart pounded and a fire he hadn't felt in a long time burned through him.

"I will not say I am sorry," he whispered in her hair.

"You have no reason to apologize." She nestled closer to him. "Neither of us do."

She showed no signs of moving but rather nestled content in his arms. The stolen minutes were precious to him, but he wouldn't compromise her.

"We had best return to your sister. She'll begin to worry."

"I know you're right. It would be best."

He released her from his arms, took her hand, and led her out of the cave.

"I'm glad you brought me here," he said before they reached her sister. "But you must not return. Not alone."

ALICIA HAD BEEN kissed before, by the baker's son. She was thirteen and thought herself an adult. At the time she didn't understand all the emotion and mystery associated with a kiss. To her, it was much like an old aunt kissing her, except the baker's boy kissed her lips.

But the captain, the tenderness of his caress made her heart skitter. His deep voice was melodious and made her wonder how he would sound singing. The taste of his lips lingered and warmed her. The realization struck her that she wouldn't have stopped him if he wanted more and if he didn't pursue it, she would have.

No, she did not regret his kiss. Nor did she want her soothing stone to quiet her feelings. Banish *these* feelings? Not at all, she'd rather prolong them as long as possible.

His firm grasp and the warmth of his hand kept her emotions high. Before he released her hand, he gave her a small intimate squeeze and her heart thundered.

They joined Beatrice, walked up the cliff path, and on toward the manor. Justin smiled and spoke with Beatrice, but it was her arm that was intertwined with his.

The walk back was much too quick for her liking. They reached the door, and he released her arm. For a moment she felt she was a ship without a rudder.

Mr. Dodd opened the door.

"Ladies." They stood in the foyer. "I can see why Lady Alicia enjoys the beach. Thank you both for your company."

"I, too, enjoyed the day," her sister said.

Justin turned to Alicia.

"I've thoroughly enjoyed my tour of Sommer-by-the-Sea." He took her hand and brought it to his lips.

"Caulfield." Elkington stood at the library door.

Justin's face paled. He pivoted toward her brother-in-law.

"Elkington, a moment in private, if I may." He reached into his breast pocket, pulled out an envelope, and handed it to him. "From Barrington."

Elkington opened the message and scanned it.

"We need to discuss this."

Justin turned to Alicia and Beatrice. "If you will excuse me."

He followed Elkington into the library and closed the door without waiting for an answer.

The sisters removed their bonnets, put down their reticules and went into the drawing room. The pungent aroma of tea and fresh bilberry tarts filled the room.

"The tarts smell delicious. Beatrice, you have outdone yourself." Alicia took a seat on the settee.

Beatrice poured the tea. "I like him, Alicia. Very much." She popped a piece of the tart into her mouth and closed her eyes. "Delicious."

"The tart or Captain Caulfield?" Alicia smirked as Beatrice's eyes flew open, her mouth full of the confection.

Her sister washed down the pastry with a few sips of tea and patted her lips with a serviette.

"You know, you are horrid. If I'm correct, you think he is…" Beatrice's eyes narrowed. "Delectable."

Alicia's mouth gaped open. She couldn't help herself as she burst out laughing. After catching her breath, she exclaimed, "I can't keep him out of my mind. Nor can I explain why I'm drawn to him. Words are my trade, yet I find none to explain what happens to me when I think about him and when I'm with him."

"Once upon a time I felt much the same." Beatrice grasped her hand and gently squeezed it. "I'm happy for you."

"Once upon a time? Do you—" Alicia ached for her sister.

"Hush. Douglas and I will come to an understanding. We are for each other and do love each other, very much." Beatrice let out a long sigh, placed a tart on a plate, and handed it to Alicia. "We will resolve this."

⇒⟫⟫⟨⟨⟨⟵

JUSTIN PACED THE library as Elkington read Barrington's message.

"You're as wound up as a caged animal. Sit down before you wear out the Aubusson. What has you so disturbed? It's not this." He held up the message.

"Your sister-in-law." He stood looking out the window but saw nothing but disaster. How did he get in such a pickle?

"I thought so. She's a fine woman. Although I'm surprised. I'm afraid she did not speak kindly of you before you met her. She has this idea that you're destroying her writing career. I dared not tell her you were a friend." Elkington unsuccessfully tried to stifle a light laugh. "I'm glad that problem is resolved."

"You don't understand." Justin pivoted. He shifted his weight from one foot to the other. He faced the enemy in situations he was sure he would die and luckily survived. Yet he never felt so vulnerable as he did now.

Elkington stared at him. His smile faded turning first to concern, then into anger.

"My god, what happened?"

"She has no idea that I'm…" The words stuck in his throat. "J. C. Melrose. I've tried to tell her several times, when we met, at the cathedral, the castle. She skillfully diverted the conversation each time."

"That's a relief," Elkington mumbled and tossed Barrington's letter onto the table. "You mean she interrupts you and takes over the conversation."

"I didn't think I was her only victim." Justin rubbed the back of his neck.

"Believe me. You're not."

"Alicia took me into her confidence and showed me the cave in spite of her fears and shared why it provoked such a deep emotion. Her tale was so vivid that I was held captive and imagined myself in the cave. I was as panicked and fearful as she had been. I thought my uncle exaggerated her ability. He was correct. Alicia Hartley is a master storyteller."

"Alicia addresses everything with passion and determination." Elkington stared at him.

"I've always faced my problems, even the difficult ones. But this, I have no idea what to do. This I will tell you. I will not walk into that reading tomorrow as J. C. Melrose. I won't humiliate her like that."

"Your choice is simple. You can take the coward's way out and not go—"

"That's not an option." Justin spit the words out.

"I didn't think so. Then you know what you must do," Elkington said.

"She will hate me. I may lose her forever." He stared at his friend and tried to swallow around the hot knot in his throat.

"No, it won't be easy, and she will be angry. You will just have to work hard to win her back. I know. Her sister is the same." Elkington put his arm on his shoulder. "Do you want me to send Alicia in?"

Justin nodded to Elkington. He had barely left when Alicia glided into the room. He took on his well-tested military mask, the one that radiated an air of calm and self-confidence to others. Inwardly he dreaded speaking to her. He took a deep breath and tried to relax.

"You wanted to speak with me?" She sat on the settee and clasped her hands in her lap. Her eyes gleamed with expectation, making his task all the worse.

He had practiced telling her in his room, on the ship, even walking with her. At the moment he couldn't recall anything he planned. He sat next to her and took her hand.

"I have something to tell you. I've tried several times, but the conversation gets diverted and we're on another topic."

"Oh, I do interrupt. If I—"

"No. That's not the issue. I've been trying to tell you that I use my mother's maiden name when I write. I thought it would be uncomfortable to use Caulfield with my uncle the publisher."

"That's understandable."

He waited for her to ask him what his pen name was, but she didn't. Did she suspect he was J. C. Melrose and wait for him to confess? He looked into her eyes. No, she was innocent and at that moment he didn't know whose heart he was breaking, hers or his.

"I write under the name of Justin Caulfield Melrose." He said it and let his name hang in the air along with his heart.

Her eyes widened. She said and did nothing.

"J. C. Melrose," she said.

"Yes." The single word was as horrid as a bullet to his chest.

She pulled her hand away, stood, and marched out of the library, slamming the door behind her.

Not a tear. Not a word. But he saw the pain and anger in her eyes, or was it hate?

His hopes crumbled and he had no one to blame but himself. He came into the manor feeling welcome, now he was an intruder. Losing Alicia was the worst loss he'd ever suffered. At the moment, he doubted he would get over it quickly, if at all.

He took up his belongings and left through the terrace door. He had every intention of spending a good part of the night drinking some of Barrington's fine French brandy.

⤞⤝

"HOW COULD HE?" She ranted at her sister and Elkington in the drawing room. "He betrayed me. Why? Is he trying to ruin me?"

She swallowed hard to hold back the tears.

Beatrice hugged her tightly and looked at her husband.

Elkington sat across from them nervously swirling sherry in his glass.

"Would you like to return to London? We can leave tomorrow if you wish it." Beatrice rocked her gently. "Or you can help me with the party. Perhaps you and Effie could arrange some entertainment."

"Thank you, but I don't need a distraction. I want to understand what I did that he has treated me so badly." Alicia sat back, her lips quivering.

Beatrice took her back into her arms. "Go ahead. It's all right to cry."

Alicia shook her head. "Crying only clouds your mind. I just want to understand why he wants to ruin me."

"I don't quite agree." Elkington put his glass down. "Alicia, who are you angry with, Justin or Anonymous? Justin did nothing more than write a book about a soldier's experience. And a damn good one at that. He wasn't on a campaign to harm you."

"You don't understand," she continued. Her throat seemed to close. "If he had told me when we met, I would have been annoyed, possibly angry. After this deception, how will I ever trust him?"

"He mentioned he tried to tell you several times, but someone kept changing the subject," Elkington said.

"Are you blaming me?" Alicia asked, her words sharper than she planned.

"No, of course not, just that he had no intention of deceiving or hurting you."

"He cares for you," Beatrice said. "As much as you do him."

Alicia's lips trembled. She gulped hard as hot tears trailed down her cheeks. She pulled away from Beatrice and stood.

"You don't understand. Neither of you do."

Alicia swung the door open and hurried to her room. By the time she reached it, her fingers hurt from rubbing her amber pendant.

CHAPTER NINE

ALICIA WOKE THE following morning having spent the night tossing and turning. She went over each meeting with Justin, each conversation. Had she run away with the exchanges and not given him an opportunity to speak? By morning she concluded he could have stopped her. Told her he was J. C. Melrose. And all of this could have been avoided.

Satisfied she had a better ending for this tragedy, she had breakfast in her room to avoid Beatrice and Elkington. It wasn't until after luncheon that she emerged for the day, wearing her new pelisse, bonnet, and carrying her book marked for the reading in her hand. She found Beatrice in the drawing room.

"We missed you at the table," Beatrice said, her needlework in hand.

"I had a terrible headache." She stopped and took a deep breath. "No, I didn't have a headache, just a terrible night's sleep."

Beatrice abandoned her stitching and gave Alicia her full attention.

"Would you like to join me? I'm meeting Mrs. Bainbridge and the others at Mrs. Miller's." Alicia stood waiting for her sister's answer.

"I was hoping you'd ask me to walk with you. Elkington went out earlier and told me he will meet us there."

They hadn't spoken a word until they were half-way to the library.

"I let him kiss me." The confession made the intimacy, less…intimate. However, the comfort that she expected from her confession didn't happen.

"I know," Beatrice said, her voice soft.

Alicia halted, shocked. Beatrice grabbed her arm and pulled her along.

"Your eyes gave you away. In addition, the captain is all you've spoken about these last few days, and you pouted over the weekend while he was away." They continued on a bit further. "You know you love him."

"I may have thought I did, but not now." She straightened her spine and continued on.

The silver bell tinkled as they entered the library.

"Lady Alicia."

Alicia turned to Marjorie Miller.

"Everything is ready. There is a great deal of excitement for this reading. Charles is putting on the finishing touches. We should be ready in a few minutes."

She smiled but wondered, why hadn't her husband mentioned who Justin was when he introduced them? Was everyone against her? She blinked and moved on from that thought.

"Come this way." Mrs. Miller brought her to the research room in the back of the library where one of the large windows was draped in dark damask. Chairs were set in lines in front of a table where books were stacked. A podium was to the side.

"Each author will read from their book. Afterwards, you'll take questions from those attending. You will have time to sign the books and bookplates."

Mrs. Miller led her to her place at the table.

"Many people have come in asking for your book. There is quite a waiting list to borrow it."

"Alicia." She turned to Effie heading toward her, Hattie, Anna, and Pat trailing behind. Mrs. Bainbridge stood with

Barrington and gave her a gracious nod.

She searched the crowd and found Beatrice with Elkington and other acquaintances, but not Justin. Surely, Mrs. Miller would have told her if he cried off. She fretted, wanting to scold him, yell at him, and kiss him all at the same time.

A tinkle of the bell announced another arrival. She smiled to herself and waited. He was here. There was no need to turn and confirm his presence. No need, but she did. Alicia lifted her gaze and found him staring at her.

He stood by himself in the middle of the crowd. How did he go unnoticed? Was everyone blind?

Even in his great coat one could detect his strength and the air of command that surrounded him. He should have been lost in the crowd of people standing in the back, but they gave him wide berth as he walked to the front of the group.

What drew her to this man? It wasn't his expressive eyes or the handsome proportions of his face or even his wide strong shoulders. It was nothing, but it was everything. The way the curl in his thick dark hair fell over his brow when he was deep in thought, his open warm smile that made her heart race, but most of all he listened to her. Not just heard her but concentrated on what she said.

His curiosity was as vast as hers was, and he eagerly entered into discussions on any topic. He spoke to her not as a simpering shadow of a person, but as an intelligent peer and wasn't intimidated. That's what made him...perfect.

Mrs. Miller approached him. She motioned toward his seat at the table, but he declined. He remained at the edge of the crowd.

Her heart ached that he didn't want to be near her. A quick disturbing thought choked her. Had she misjudged him? Did he want the attention all for himself? Was all her dreaming just that, dreams?

Get up and leave, the little voice in her head said.

But she wasn't a coward. Alicia took a deep breath and opened her book. She looked down at the page she marked to read, the hero and heroine's first encounter. Alicia made a quick decision and leafed through the pages until she found the passage she sought. Satisfied, she slipped in her bookmark, clasped her hands in front of her, and waited.

Several moments later, Mrs. Miller came to the podium.

"Ladies and Gentlemen. I'm Mrs. Miller, and I would like to welcome you to the Sommer Circulating Library. Before we begin our program for today, I have a few announcements. Those of you who have books that are due, please return them to the desk. Others are waiting to read them. We have received new books which many of you have requested." She took out a list. "We now have *Mansfield Park*, *The Wanderer*, *The Towers of Ravenswold*, and *Waverley*. They are available at the new books table across from the desk.

"Today is our monthly author presentation in which authors read passages from their stories and answer your questions. We're happy to launch the autumn season with our annual Sommer Literary Harvest Salon this evening. Our guest authors are attending. We invite you to join us tonight when we can share the evening with them and ask questions about their stories, their research, and any other information they are willing to divulge."

A mild chuckle spread through the group.

"Those of you who attend every month are aware that we host one author. Today we're most fortunate to have two writers with us. I would like to introduce our first author whose books are popular. J. C. Melrose." Mrs. Miller motioned to Justin in the crowd. He gave a quick nod to polite applause.

"His book, *In My Brother's Shadow* tells the story of one man's survival in unspeakable wartime conditions. The hero, Captain James Callum Mallory has a mission to complete while keeping his men safe. Losing a man is not a choice. The tale is about the decisions the captain must make and what it costs him. His series is dedicated to those who fought in any war, to let them know they are understood, and that they are not alone. It is Mr.

Melrose's hope that for those who did not serve his stories provide an inside perspective of what war, leadership and the consequence of decisions, and sacrifices are like as well as what is left of a man when he returns. My husband, who is a retired officer has read all of Mr. Melrose's stories and says they are vibrant and accurate. Mr. Melrose."

A soft murmur spread through the room.

Justin read the opening chapter of his book. His deep baritone voice punctuated with emotion kept the story vivid and alive. There was no denying his talent, not that she wanted to. Oddly enough, she was proud of him. When he closed his book, the attendees enthusiastically applauded.

"Thank you, Mr. Melrose. You all have met our next author, Lady Alicia Hartley. She and her family are long-time residents of Sommer-by-the-Sea and we're excited to have her join us today."

Alicia tilted her head in acknowledgement to slightly louder applause, mostly from Effie and her other friends.

"Lady Alicia's book, *The Lost Dowry*, presents a picture of a woman whose goal is the wellbeing of her family. Her story is about a family who falls on hard times and faces the decision of grabbing her happiness or sacrificing it for her family. Her heroine Clarissa must make decisions and give her family the tools they need to succeed. Lady Alicia's books are highly sought after for the way her heroines, bluestockings of sorts, are women that break society's dictates to reach their goals and the price they must pay to succeed. I have read her stories. She puts her heroines in situations many women face and writes them a plan to succeed. She is an inspiration. Lady Alicia."

Alicia nodded to Mrs. Miller and opened her book.

She briefly hesitated before she started her passage, tempted to go back to her first choice, but decided against it.

Easily lost in her words, she read with passion and emotion. The room was silent when she finished. Justin stepped forward and applauded loud and long. Others around him joined in.

"Lady Alicia." She turned to Charles Miller. "Your writing is exquisite. So descriptive. You tore out my heart. I didn't want you to stop. You created a woman who is strong and demands not to be ignored. She was unafraid and faced her challenges head on."

Alicia looked at Justin as he stood nodding in agreement. The room was abuzz.

Justin took his seat at her side as Mrs. Miller created a line for people to have books or bookplates signed. They stood back and listened to Mrs. Miller's instructions.

"Well done, Lady Alicia."

She glanced at his hesitant gaze and turned away.

"Betrayal of a friend. It is a difficult subject, but you handled it with precision."

Had she gone too far? If she hadn't, why did she regret speaking her truth?

"I don't know how or if ever I can make amends. And I'm telling you this now, here, because I was concerned if I told you privately you would turn me away. I couldn't stand that."

This wasn't the place to continue this conversation. But he was correct, she wouldn't speak to him but not for the reasons he thought. What would she say, *All is forgiven? Why didn't you tell me? How could you kiss me?* Most of all, *Why did you make me fall in love with you?*

Her heart leaped to her throat. Love him. Her mind reeled. Alicia searched the crowd for Beatrice. She was by Elkington and Barrington, watching her. A perfect smile spread on her face saying, *It took you long enough.*

Thankfully, someone stood in front of her and handed her a book plate to sign. Relieved, she smiled, asked them their name, listened to their compliment, and thanked them from her heart.

An hour later, Effie and her other friends were the last on her line. She glanced at Justin's line. People were waiting to speak to him.

"We're here to celebrate your wonderful success. Come, we're off to the tearoom."

Alicia said her good-bye to Mr. and Mrs. Miller. With all her heart she wanted to tell Justin he was right. She wouldn't have listened to him. With Effie and the others pestering her to leave, she didn't have time to say anything. Perhaps tonight at the Harvest Salon. At the moment, she allowed her friends to pull her away and left without saying a word to him.

CHAPTER TEN

JUSTIN STARED AT his reflection in the carriage window. Earlier, while preparing for the evening, he examined his image as he fussed with his cravat, tugged the front of his crème color waistcoat until the garment sat correctly and he slipped into his tailcoat. Now he saw that his fine clothes didn't hide the man beneath them. He had killed men without regret yet the hurt in her eyes tore at him. Well, there was nothing for him to do.

"Charles Miller gave you a fine review," Barrington said as the carriage made its way to the library.

Justin turned and gave him his attention.

"Yes, he is a good man. When I was here last year, I went to Edinburgh to speak with his cousin and her son. Lawson told me she remarried and moved to Glasgow."

"You can't take the place of every fallen soldier. You went above and beyond commanding your men, leading them, and have seen the families of every one of those in our regiment that have fallen. I asked you to console them, not see to their futures."

"I spoke to women and their children that were left without anything. They're fortunate if their families could take them in. A kind word, encouragement, an introduction cost me nothing but meant so much to them."

"You've spent the last years taking care of everyone but yourself. Perhaps it's time for you to settle down."

"That's a surprising statement from you. I never thought you a hypocrite." He turned to the window, past his reflection at the darkening sky.

"I have my lady in sight and have for some time. Ours is a long game, but worth it. Ah, here we are. Just in time to avoid your interrogation." They got out of the carriage and entered the library.

The room had been transformed. The furniture was moved to the perimeter. The seating, set into groups, created small areas for conversations. Vases full of greens and fall flowers along with artfully fashioned garlands decorated the room. A log burned in the fireplace, and punch and light refreshments were set out on the desk.

He didn't recall the last time he attended a London party, but this event had the same atmosphere of anticipation. He turned from Barrington to survey the room.

He found her at once and made up his mind he would not accept defeat. Barrington was correct. Alicia was worth fighting for. With nothing to lose, he headed toward her.

"Elkington, Lady Elkington," he nodded and turned to Alicia. "Lady Alicia."

"Captain… Mr. Melrose. What should I call you?"

"Alicia, really," her sister hissed.

He stared into her eyes, not surprised that her words echoed his own thoughts. The woman did not hide her feelings nor was she going to make this easy. She may have won this skirmish, but he was determined to win the war.

"Well deserved. You never disappoint, do you? Caulfield will do." He turned to Elkington and his wife. "If you will excuse us."

He threaded Alicia's arm through his, hoping she wouldn't remain planted in place and have him tugging her around the room. To his relief she went willingly.

"When I read your story earlier this week," she said after several minutes, "I imagined I was with Captain Mallory."

His chest swelled at her good opinion of his work.

"But the people and places came alive when you read today. I thought about your reading later and wanted to speak to you about your use of words—"

"Captain Caulfield, Lady Alicia." He schooled his face not to show his annoyance at the intrusion. If he had seen anyone approach, he would have avoided the encounter.

"Mr. Hawkins." Alicia turned to him. "Captain Caulfield, this is Ernest Hawkins, the editor and proprietor of the newspaper, the *Sommer Sentinel*."

He lifted his chin, the corner of his mouth raised. Justin acknowledged the man with a curt nod.

"Mr. Hawkins."

"Captain, I'm honored to meet you. I read your series. They can get your heart racing. Are all the actions taken from the battlefield?"

A group of people gathered around him and Alicia.

"I use my experiences as a basis for my writing. Some scenes are as I remember. Other times I cobble together pieces from different campaigns to make my point."

"Do you ever take a victory and turn it into a loss?"

"Never." He was quiet, yet his voice contained a strong suggestion of rebuke. "Mr. Hawkins, I won't discredit the victories any of the men so valiantly earned. It is unfortunate, but there are enough lost campaigns to choose from."

"I... I apologize, Captain. I didn't mean any disrespect to you or the men. I thought as a fiction writer..." Hawkins' perception of fiction was not unexpected but disturbing just the same. He let the man stew a bit longer.

"Your apology is accepted," he said, smiling smoothly, betraying nothing of his annoyance.

"Alicia, if you please." He turned to a young woman standing next to Alicia.

"Euphemia, let me introduce you to Captain Justin Caulfield. Captain Caulfield, may I present my good friend Lady Euphemia Brandt."

He smiled at Euphemia with no trace of his former displeasure.

"The primary characters in both your stories jump off the page. They are real, yet the stories are different. How does an author create characters with such realism from pen and ink?"

"A writer needs to understand human tendencies and how they affect their character, their skills, knowledge, behavior, eating, communication, and intimacy." A soft whisper rippled through the people standing around them at Alicia's words.

Several of the matrons appeared horrified, others laughed nervously. He drew her hand closer, bringing her a step nearer to him.

"People respond in their own unique way, especially when societal constraints are layered onto the interaction. I admit to being a bit of a rebel." Alicia was a woman of her convictions. She didn't make any excuses. "My stories take romanticism a bit past women who are intelligent and resourceful."

He noticed the confused expressions from the people around them. A glance at Alicia and he knew it was all she needed to go on.

"My stories delve into the difference between men and woman, what drives them, and I don't mean any obvious physical differences," Alicia said.

"I agree, Lady Alicia." He looked at her with approval.

Euphemia turned to Justin, as did the others standing with them.

"A man's first reaction when faced with an issue is to make the problem go away. We have a tendency to act first." Soft laughter spread through the crowd, which was made up mainly of women.

"Yes, and while men may take immediate action," Alicia said, "women organize and plan. We may take longer to reach our conclusion, but it's with more satisfying results."

"In everything?" Effie asked with a mischievous smile brightening her eyes.

He turned his head and stared at the daring Effie. He had no doubt where her mind was going.

"It's possible," Alicia said without hesitation. "Men tend to react with their body while women react first with their mind. A writer can use that knowledge to create characters that appear real. It's not only the reaction, but the emotion, the movement, the conflict surrounding the reaction. Breaking those expectations also creates conflict, and isn't that why we read? To see how the characters manage their challenges."

Some in the group nodded and were deep in thought, while others had a glazed look. "I strongly believe authentic characters can be created when the author is aware of the way people may react."

"Mr. Melrose, where did you serve?"

He responded to the military questions, relieved at the change of topic. The questions were the same wherever he went.

Did he cross paths with their relatives or neighbors that served with Wellington? In most cases, he did not. Those people went away disappointed.

The crowd around them dwindled and they walked on.

"I applaud your response to Lady Euphemia," he said as they continued around the room. "You were tactful. I, veering from my normal male approach to things, stopped to organize my thoughts, plan what to say. You surprised me with taking action first."

She bit the side of her cheek to stop from smiling.

"Lady Euphemia made a good observation. Our stories are very different, yet both are good. Writers can't please every reader."

She hesitated in the middle of the room. He found himself enjoying the discussion and coaxed her along. He had more to say on the topic.

"Readers have their preferences," he said. "Some like mystery, some war stories, and others romance. Our stories for instance. Your readers devour your descriptions and the strong female characters you meticulously create. For my readers, I deliver the spontaneity of battles, putting them in the midst of the actions where they experience what the fighting men face."

"I agree. Both our stories can exist independently and peaceably."

Pleased with himself, he patted her hand on his arm. They continued to greet people and answer their questions until her friends whisked her away.

He made his way through the large double doors in the back of the library, into the adjoining research room, and faced a large palladium window that looked out at the harbor.

The research tables were arranged end to end in front of the window forming a grand buffet. Draped in fine white linen, the tables were set with supper.

Mrs. Miller served a sumptuous supper with sliced chicken, glazed salmon, and roasted carrots. A variety of cheeses, including some from Wiltshire, were set out, as well as baskets of breads and rolls along with butter and jams.

Confectionery items were laid out on one end of the table: shortbread, apple tarts, bilberry tarts, ices, and trifle.

White wine, sweet madeira, as well as cups filled with ratafia, sweet cordial flavored with fruit and almonds, were arranged on the table.

"You two look well together," Barrington took a poured cup of negus from the table.

Justin gave him a questioning glance.

His friend laughed. "Why are you surprised? The only person you choose to walk with is Lady Alicia. Granted, she is quite becoming and charming."

"The woman is much more than 'quite becoming and charming.' She is intelligent and creative."

"Are you trying to convince me or yourself?"

Justin glared at Barrington.

"Your comment isn't worth a response." Justin downed the negus in one swallow.

"I didn't expect one. I asked the question to make you think, be honest with yourself."

He put his empty cup down while he looked across the room and said nothing.

"Here." Barrington picked up a filled cup and handed it to him.

"What is this for?" Justin looked at the cup as if he had never seen anything like it before.

"Lady Alicia is standing by herself." Barrington leaned close to him. "Bring her the refreshment and say something nice to her. Need I give you more instructions or should I make that an order?"

Justin swung his head in her direction and without another word made his way to her.

"Lady Alicia." She gave him a nondescript smile, the type she gave to everyone. He should have let Barrington give her the cup. This was turning into a battle.

"You appeared parched." He handed her the refreshment.

Surprise lit her face for a moment before she recovered. She took the offered drink, sipped, and gave him a dazzling smile, the one he had longed to see.

"You have my thanks." She took another longer drink. "I've been answering questions all evening."

"Would you like to take another turn or two of the room and ward off your admirers for a short while." He didn't offer his arm, but waited for her consent. What would happen if she didn't accept his offer?

Thinking better of his tactic, he went on the offensive. He removed the empty cup from her hand, placed it on the tray of a passing barmaid, and laced her arm through his.

"YOU SURPRISE ME, Captain Caulfield. You broke the rules."

"I've had a very good teacher, Lady Alicia." Justin's self-satisfied grin made her smile.

"A turn or two of the room would be lovely." The last thing she wanted was to be angry with him. He was correct. They weren't competitors.

No. She didn't want to be angry at him. They developed a closeness she reserved for her sister, Mrs. Bainbridge, and Effie. No subject was forbidden. She let him into that secret place and didn't want to close him out.

He steered them between the bookshelves along the wall that contained the classics. They weren't quite alone, but far enough from others for a private conversation.

"Is this an apology?" she asked, with a confident grin.

"No. Not an apology."

She looked crestfallen.

"I had no intention of deceiving you. I tried several times to tell you I am J. C. Melrose, the day we met in London and here at the library. You had a poor impression of me, well... at least of my pen name. I knew you wouldn't consider speaking to me, much less spend time with me, if I disclosed I was J. C. Melrose. When you didn't give me a chance to tell you the truth, I seized the opportunity for you to judge me for who I am."

Her thoughtful expression encouraged him.

"Do you disagree?" he asked.

She plucked a book from the shelf and handed the volume to him.

He looked at the title: *Julius Caesar*. Was she tormenting him? Not from the expression on her face.

He searched the bindings until he found what he wanted and handed her a book.

"Rather than Brutus, I prefer—"

"Mark Antony, of course." Her light laugh made him smile and she put *Antony and Cleopatra* back in their place and turned to him. "You're right. You did try to tell me. I also agree, we are not competitors."

His expression turned sensual. Heat rushed up her neck and onto her cheeks.

"About not giving J. C. Melrose a chance…" She took his arm and started toward the refreshments. "Punch sounds good right now."

They strolled across the room.

"Mrs. Bainbridge, may I introduce you to Captain Justin Caulfield. He writes as J. C. Melrose."

"It's a pleasure to meet you. I enjoyed your reading."

"You have my thanks." He nodded graciously.

"Lord Barrington mentioned that your portrayals of the battles are precise and accurate. He has often spoken about your stories," Mrs. Bainbridge said.

"I thought both readings were enjoyable," Effie said, joining them, Charles Miller at her side. "I found it fascinating that the leading characters in each book had similar problems but weren't portrayed the same way. Captain Mallory was in a battle, as was Clarisse. I wonder what stories you would create if you wrote each other's story?"

"That's an interesting notion," Mrs. Bainbridge said. "However… what if they took the same story plot and each wrote in their style? That would be a wonderful exercise."

Standing by the newspaper rack, Effie pulled the recent edition out, closed her eyes and pointed to the page.

Everyone looked over her shoulder.

"Missing Walmer Castle Chest Found – Empty?"

She turned to Justin and Alicia. "Should I dare you both to write a short story based on this headline?"

"Interesting challenge. Captain Caulfield?" Alicia asked.

"Are you serious?" he asked. All three women nodded.

"I see I'm outnumbered. A good soldier knows when to give way."

"Who will judge the work?" Effie asked.

"If you like, I will," Charles said. "I'm looking forward to reading the stories."

"May the best story win," Alicia said.

CHAPTER ELEVEN

"I ENJOYED SEEING Caulfield. You know this book of his is quite good." Elkington went back to reading.

"Why didn't you tell me you knew Isaac Caulfield?" Alicia picked her head up from the newspaper.

"Why would I?" He kept reading.

"I find it strange that you suggested I contact him about publishing my story but made no mention of your association with him." She observed his reaction carefully.

"Do you believe I interfered with your negotiation?" He kept reading.

How did Beatrice deal with this man? How he was able to read and have a conversation at the same time was beyond her.

"The thought did cross my mind." She bent over the newspaper.

"I didn't mention you or my connection to the Hartley family to Isaac or Justin. I assure you, Isaac evaluated your story and made his decision strictly on the quality of your work." Elkington looked up. "You didn't mention me to him, did you?"

"Of course not. What would I say? Good day, Mr. Caulfield. Let me tell you about my very self-important brother-in-law."

Elkington laughed and returned to his book. Beatrice entered the room. She handed Alicia a message.

"This came for you in the post. I knew that robin egg blue

would be perfect on you," Beatrice said as she sat and took up her needlework.

"I thought Mrs. Miller's salon was quite nice."

"Of course you did. Your bilberry apple tart won first prize again," Elkington said. "I'm looking forward to enjoying them." He went back to his reading.

A flash of humor crossed Beatrice's face. She turned to her sister. "What is this challenge you and Captain Caulfield have taken on?"

"There was a challenge? What happened? Is it a duel at dawn? Do you need a second?" Elkington put his book down and focused on the conversation.

"Nothing so dramatic. A *writing* challenge. The idea came from Mrs. Bainbridge and Effie." Alicia glanced at the envelope and gave her attention to Elkington. "She mentioned the lead characters in both my story and the captain's faced similar problems, yet we dealt with them differently. She was curious what our stories would be like if we wrote about the same incident."

"Sounds interesting. What incident did you choose?" Elkington pursed his lips and nodded.

"Effie picked the topic from the headline." She held up the paper and showed him the front page. "I'm reading Mr. Hawkins' editorial to find something on which to base my story. He quotes people he's interviewed and asks if they can solve the mystery. I wish someone would edit his work. This is atrocious. He mentions gold, thieves giving coins to the poor, free traders, the English blockade, spies. These are the ones that are believable. The others are not plausible. Here is one about a ghost taking the gold."

"I heard everyone is laughing about that theory. What would a ghost want with gold?" Beatrice continued with her needlework.

"I'm attracted to the idea of giving the gold to people in need. Mr. Hawkins doesn't say much here, although he poses lots of theories."

"That's a relief. I thought you were going to say smugglers."

"Why would you choose smugglers?" she asked.

"A 'free trader' is another term for a smuggler who breaks through a blockade."

"Excuse me, m'lord. A messenger. He says it is urgent." Giles waited for Elkington to respond.

"Have them wait in the library." He put the book on the side table and rose. As he passed Beatrice he caressed her chin, kissed her brow, and left the room.

Beatrice let out a deep sigh, staring at the door. "You were right. The gift wasn't necessary. All we needed to do was listen to each other." She took up her needlework yet again. "I love him so much."

"I never doubted that for a moment." Alicia was deeply relieved Beatrice and Elkington were reconciled.

She returned to reading Hawkins' article with renewed interest. After several minutes she put the paper down, knocking the letter Beatrice gave her onto the floor. She retrieved it. As she sat up, a contented smile spread across her face.

"This story is not about the stolen gold at all." Her mind was jumping from one idea to another. Her thoughts came together, and a plan took shape.

"What do you mean?" Beatrice asked without missing a stitch.

"I have no idea what the captain is writing. I suspect sailing and brandy." Her mouth twisted into a cynical grin. "Mine will deal with smugglers."

"Dearest," her sister said, putting down her needlework. "What do you know about that awful business?"

"I'm an author. I'll find something." She held the envelope and tapped a corner on the table.

She looked at it, startled by the sender: Caulfield Publishing. Perhaps he wanted to offer for her next book. She opened and read the note.

Dear Lady Alicia Hartley,

I hope your trip to Sommer-by-the-Sea was uneventful. You will be pleased to know that orders have been arriving for The Lost Dowry *as well as other books in your series.*

By now you're aware of the news. I tried to tell you several times when you were last here, but you were so upset. You didn't listen. I'm glad the way everything has resolved and I'm sure there is no impediment in any way.

Mrs. Caulfield and I are traveling to Alnwick and plan to stop at Sommer-by-the-Sea. I would like to speak to you and my nephew Captain Caulfield. We should arrive by the end of the week.

Isaac Caulfield

She had no idea what he was talking about. What would he want to tell her? She'd find out soon enough.

Elkington returned, took his seat, and picked up his book as if nothing had happened.

"You'll be happy to know, Elkington, that Mr. Caulfield – the publisher, not the captain – is coming to Sommer-by-the-Sea later this week. You can renew your acquaintance."

He didn't move but she saw him try to stifle a grin.

The mantel clock struck the hour.

"I must dash. I'm meeting Effie at the Sommer Inn. Beatrice, I'll be back in plenty of time to help with the plans for the Harvest Party."

Alicia donned her new robin's egg blue pelisse that coordinated with her dress and bonnet. She made sure her small journal and pencil were in her reticule. As an afterthought, she removed the page from the newspaper and added it to her small bag. Satisfied she had everything, she left the house for the Sommer Inn.

The heroine of this story had to be strong and capable, a match for the captain's hero. That would mean she had to be courageous and have the ability to defend herself. This would be quite a different heroine than any of her others and the idea appealed to her. This story would take her heroine out of the ballroom, home, shop, or schoolroom. She would be fearless and intelligent.

She walked along the river as threads of a story swirled in her head. Alicia stood at the bridge, staring as the agitated river swept by.

A name? Elizabeth. No, that was too spirited a name.

Helen? That wouldn't work either. The name had to have substance.

Olivia. Yes, Olivia Fitzwilliam. She covered her mouth with her hand to stifle her laughter. A strong surname to signify her feistiness.

She crossed the bridge and came down King's Way. The inn was up ahead. Perhaps she'd even give the woman the trace of a Scottish accent. Olivia Fitzwilliam would be a challenge for any man, but especially for… Hugh Talbot.

"Good day to you, Lady Alicia."

Alicia came out of her daydreaming and found Mr. Hawkins greeting her as they both walked up the path to the Sommer Inn.

"I enjoyed the passage you read at the library." He held the door open for her. "Have you ever thought of becoming a journalist? Your insight and ability to tell a compelling story makes you a good candidate."

"No. I have never thought of journalism."

"I am sincere." He stopped by the dining room door. "I planned to speak to you for some time. You confirmed my idea when I heard you read. Working for the *Sommer Sentinel* will give you prestige. Think of the many people who would know your name."

She didn't want to brag, but her books had a wider circulation than the *Sommer Sentinel*. People, many people, already knew her name.

"You'd research and write for the paper. I'd edit your work, make it acceptable for publication…"

Alicia listened but didn't hear the rest of what Mr. Hawkins said. He would edit her work and make it acceptable for publication, and anything he edited would be attributed to him. She would be flattered by his proposal if it wasn't insulting.

"You present an interesting proposal. I'm glad we met today. I have a question about an article you published earlier this week." She opened her reticule, removed the news article, and handed it to him.

"What interests you, the idea that ghosts stole the gold?"

"That's a ridiculous theory. Everyone laughed at that idea."

Hawkins' smile collapsed at her cut.

"I'm interested in the free traders."

"There isn't much more to say. All the information is here." He folded the paper and returned it to her. "This is not something for a lady's delicate ears."

Alicia stepped to the doorway of the dining room. *Please, Effie. Don't be late today.* She scanned the dining room, relieved to find her friend sitting at a table by the front window with a pot of tea on the table.

"Welcome Lady Alicia." Mr. Perkins, the owner and manager of the inn greeted her. "Lady Euphemia is at your favorite table. This way please."

"If you will excuse me, Mr. Hawkins." She began to follow Mr. Perkins.

"You will consider my proposal?" Mr. Hawkins called after her.

"I will have to decline at this time. I have a contract for several books with my publisher and couldn't give the paper the proper time it deserves."

Alicia couldn't get away from the man quick enough. Men. Thick. Self-important. She would have to find the information she needed to win the challenge elsewhere.

CHAPTER TWELVE

"I'VE NEVER SEEN you this angry. What did Mr. Hawkins say to you?" Effie asked, glancing at the man as he waited for Mr. Perkins to direct him to a table.

Alicia took a seat and put her reticule in her lap. She poured her tea, didn't bother with the lump of sugar, and held the cup.

"Too bad we don't have any brandy. It may improve your disposition," Effie said and freshened her cup with more tea. She glanced at the biscuit on Alicia's saucer and looked away.

"Would you like the biscuit or one from the box on your lap?" Alicia asked.

"The box is for Mrs. Bainbridge." Effie put the box on the table.

"Mr. Hawkins enjoyed my reading. He thought I would be an excellent journalist and an asset to his newspaper." Alicia shook her head.

Effie gave her a stare.

"I would research and write the articles." Alicia took a sip of tea, gave the cup a disdainful glare, and added a lump of sugar.

"That isn't enough to raise your hackles. What else was in his proposal?" Effie sat back. Alicia glanced in her direction. Her friend was enjoying her annoyance.

"He would edit and make sure what I wrote was appropriate. Once he made it acceptable, he would publish it in the paper."

She stopped, let out a deep breath, and took another sip of tea.

Effie sat forward. "You're mean, Alicia Hartley. What *else* did he say?"

"It isn't what he said, but what he didn't say. He would publish it under his name." She waved her hand, banishing Hawkins' proposal. "That is not important. I asked him about his editorial. He told me the article contains all the necessary information and 'this is not something for a lady's delicate ears.' He had the audacity to be insulted I declined his generous offer."

"You shouldn't be surprised." Effie picked up Alicia's biscuit.

Alicia took the article out of her reticule. "I need to find out more about these free traders."

"Why? You're writing a romance story." Effie returned the confection to her plate uneaten and pulled her chair closer to Alicia.

"I'm sure Captain Caulfield is more familiar with spies than I am. It's first-hand knowledge that makes his stories come alive. I want to win this challenge. To do that, I need more information about the subject." She opened the paper and scanned the article with Effie reading over her shoulder. "Mr. Hawkins does mention several people. I'll interview them."

"He mentioned three gentlemen." Effie pulled the paper closer to her, almost taking it out of Alicia's hands.

"Commander Matthew Terrell."

"I met the commander. He is formerly of the Royal Navy and an older eligible bachelor. Beatrice had made sure I met him, although Elkington was less enthusiastic. He had attended a ball at the Barringtons' home in London when he was the Acting Governor of a small British colony off the coast of Germany… Saint… something. I can't recall the name at the moment."

"If you can't speak to him, perhaps your brother-in-law or Barrington would have the information you need. If Terrell was at the Barringtons' home, he would have spoken with them."

"Perhaps Elkington. Barrington was still convalescing."

Effie pointed to a paragraph in the middle of the piece. Alicia took the paper from her.

"Judge Scofield."

"The judge and my father are longtime friends." Alicia put the paper down and stared at Effie. "The last person mentioned is Mr. Perkins."

They both turned toward the reception area and stared.

"What does he have to do with this?" Effie asked.

Alicia removed her reticule from her lap, stood, and straightened her skirt.

"What are you doing?" Effie asked, with a bit of panic in her voice.

"I'm going to find out what Mr. Perkins knows about stolen gold and ghosts." Alicia patted her hand. "Enjoy your tea and leave me some biscuits. I shan't be long."

Alicia squared her shoulders and glided across the room to Mr. Perkins.

"Lady Alicia. I hope Mr. Hawkins didn't upset you?"

She didn't miss the concern in his eyes. "I assure you all is well. Why do you ask?"

"You looked a bit desperate to find Lady Euphemia and Hawkins can be, well, since he took over the *Sommer Sentinel* from his father, the paper has become a gossip sheet with little substance."

"I'll keep that in mind. I wanted to speak to you about a gift for my brother-in-law. I noticed he's been drinking sherry and not his preferred brandy. I was hoping you could perhaps help me. I wanted to surprise him with a bottle or two. He likes it so." She shamefully gave him an innocent glance, hoping to put him at ease.

"You needn't worry about Captain Elkington. I had three bottles sent to your residence this morning."

"Elkington?" She lifted her head at hearing Perkins' accusation. Elkington had broken the law? "I'll have to choose another gift."

She started to return to her table but hesitated. "I'm researching a new story, creating a place much like Sommer-by-the-Sea. The story in the *Sommer Sentinel* spurred the idea of creating a hero who is a free trader."

Mr. Perkins smiled broadly and stepped closer to her. "You can, of course, pattern him after me."

They both laughed.

"I will keep you in mind. In this story, he sails into the harbor and docks. I don't know how he will remove the contraband without being arrested."

"Lady Alicia, it is not too difficult. Free traders don't dock in the harbor and unload contraband. They take the cargo off at night in a secluded area in order not to be seen. Or if a ship is carrying illegal goods, it is lured onto the rocks."

"Lured? On purpose?"

Mr. Perkins glanced around them. He drew closer and spoke in a conspiratorial tone.

"Ships carrying highly taxed goods are targets of smugglers. Thieves steal the goods, then sell them to people. The people don't pay the tax and the smugglers don't pay for the goods. Everyone wins."

Alicia lifted her chin and stared at him. She had never thought how everyone benefited.

"Some go out at night and bring horses along the jetties that reach out from shore. They tie lanterns to them and lure the ships to the rocks."

"They intentionally wreck ships. But sailors can lose their lives."

"Some smugglers may appear to be gentlemen, but I assure you they are ruthless. There is money to be had in smuggling and they will stop at nothing. The lives of a few sailors don't matter to them."

She nodded, speechless. Such attitudes toward life were foreign to her.

"Once the ship is wrecked, they go aboard and take whatever they find as quickly as possible. Most come prepared and have carts waiting to carry off their prize." He moved away from her. "I've told you enough. Lady Alicia, be careful who you speak to about smugglers. After what was in the newspaper, people may not understand you're doing research. They may think you're doing much more. For the revenuers."

"What people?" She was aghast that anyone she knew would take part in illegal activities.

"More people than you imagine. Please. Don't get involved. These men are ruthless."

"Lady Alicia. What a pleasant surprise." Alicia's eyes widened. She turned at the greeting, her hand at her throat.

"Commander Terrell?" She let out a deep breath.

"Forgive me if I startled you," he said.

"No, please forgive me. I just read your name in the paper and was telling my friend Lady Euphemia..." She gestured toward Effie. "That you were an acquaintance."

He turned toward Effie and acknowledged her with a congenial nod.

"How are your sister and brother-in-law? It has been some time since I last saw them."

"They are quite well."

"And congratulations on your writing success. You had mentioned you enjoyed reading, so it did not surprise me when I heard you had become a great author."

"You're kind. I'm doing research on a story now. Perhaps you can help. As the Lieutenant Governor of St. Evaristus Island" – *that* was the place – "Would you be familiar with smugglers?"

"That's not a subject I would expect to find in a book written by a woman such as yourself."

She strained to keep a pleasant smile on her face. Why did every man who spoke to her think she was incapable, or that shouldn't be writing about smugglers?

"You found me out. That is my strategy. Provide my readers with a story on a subject they're not expecting. My hero is a smuggler. Any information you have would be helpful."

"Smugglers have been made to appear more attractive or interesting than they really are. These men are a rough lot. Quite ruthless and deadly."

"There's that word again."

"Word, Lady Alicia?"

"Ruthless. It is what Mr. Perkins said. In my research, I found that some smugglers wreck ships to steal the cargo. Did that happen on your island?"

"No. Smugglers moored their ships at our town dock. They looked like any other trader."

"I mean no disrespect, but you sound as if you condone smuggling."

"Not at all. Everything was imported onto St. Evaristus. With the blockades, opportunists found they could profit by importing those goods that were difficult to obtain. Not all free traders were smugglers. Most were honest hardworking seamen.

"Our port city was active and a welcome place for free traders. It was the items with high tariffs that were targets for smugglers. That is where they made their profits. At times it was difficult on the island to sort the villains from the villagers."

"The villagers must be aware smuggling is illegal. They would help capture these men. The villagers must help, testify to their activity," she said.

"Of course, they are well aware it's wrong to trade in contraband items, but these men are smart. That is why they prosper. As to reporting the activity… what activity? The smugglers insist the villagers turn away so they can rightly claim they saw nothing, making identification impossible. The criminal might be one of their neighbors. Money is to be made in all aspects of smuggling, from the theft, the transport of the goods, to providing desired goods to the villagers and paying them to be silent."

"The smugglers risk their lives for money," she said.

"Not all free traders are enticed by the money, although it is difficult to not take it. Some people are smugglers for the excitement, the adventure."

He glanced over her head at the doorway.

"Terrell, will your lady friend be joining us?" Alicia didn't recognize the man, but she responded to his insolent gaze with a cold, hard stare.

"If only I were with this lovely lady." Terrell smiled.

"You have been most generous with your time and information." She nodded to the commander, ready to return to Effie.

"Will I play a part in your story?" The mischief in his eyes made her smile. His playfulness softened his hard look and made him more appealing, something she hadn't been aware of before.

"The dashing hero?" she teased.

"Oh no. The dastardly villain." He chuckled at his words. "I admire your resourcefulness, but I would choose another topic for your story. A romance between a lovely lady and an admirer perhaps. I will guarantee a romance would be safer. Smugglers interest no one."

She said goodbye and made her way back to Effie. She felt his eyes on her back and shivered. He hadn't changed since their first introduction.

"That was enlightening. Smuggling may be against the law, but the free traders have a way of compelling villagers to cooperate with them, or at least not take any action that will get them convicted. So far, everyone has warned me away from the topic."

"Which makes it all the more alluring," Effie said.

"Precisely." Alicia took a sip of tea. Her lips pinched at the tepid liquid. She freshened her cup. Olivia and Hugh. He is a smuggler and she is…

"You are enjoying this challenge. Does it have anything to do with Captain Caulfield?" Effie knew better than to look her in her eye, the coward.

"I'm as good a writer as he is, and I do enjoy challenges."

"And conquests."

Alicia's head popped up. Effie gave her a smug glare.

"I have no idea what you're talking about. Captain Caulfield is the nephew of my publisher. I have to be cordial to him."

A small smile tugged at the corners of Effie's mouth. "The man is besotted with you. Even I can see that."

"Oh please." Alicia, in a snit, started to gather her things, stood, and faced Effie. "Are you ready?"

Effie got to her feet, picked up the box of biscuits, and gazed at the uneaten confection she left on Alicia's plate. Before Alicia turned to leave, she reached for it and handed it to her with a smile.

Effie started to speak but changed her mind.

"Besotted, as in, infatuated?" Seeing the surprise in Effie's face, Alicia laughed.

"Most definitely." With clear determination, Effie popped the biscuit in her mouth as they walked out of the inn. "I'm assisting Anna with her students. Where are you off to next?"

"I promised Beatrice I would help her with the plans for the Harvest Party. I do want to speak to Judge Scofield. I practically pass his office on my way home," Alicia said.

"You don't need to justify where you're going to me. His office is four streets out of your way. You won't simply 'pass' it." Effie's infectious laugh bubbled up. "Tell me what you find out."

"I'll return to the manor after I clear my head and put this plot together. Will you be at Mrs. Bainbridge's for tea?"

"Yes." She raised the box in her hand. "I'm bringing the biscuits. Don't be late."

"I won't. But set aside a biscuit for me."

Effie went north toward King's Lane, while Alicia headed east toward the beach and the judge's office.

Beatrice had all the plans for the harvest party well in hand. Today they were to review the responses and confirm the menu. But at the moment that was a distraction. She needed to focus on gathering information for her story.

She passed the Town Hall and went across the lane to Scofield's office.

"Lady Alicia is here, sir." The judge's secretary gave way and let Alicia pass.

Scofield rose and greeted her. "This is a surprise. Please. Be seated." He indicated a chair in front of his desk, then settled into his chair and moved his papers away. "Will your parents be in Sommer-by-the-Sea for this year's festival? I do enjoy when they sing, and we all join in."

"They should be arriving soon. I would hate to suffer through the festival without them, and you, of course. Who else will I dance with?"

"I assure you your dance card will be filled. Should I reserve my dance now?"

"I will always have room to dance with you. I still remember my excitement when you asked me to take the floor with you at my first dance."

"You stood on my shoes as we danced around." The judge chuckled. "You were all of six years old. I'm happy you've stopped for a visit… but I'm sure there is a reason you're here."

"I'm doing research for my new story. I need more details. The story is based on an editorial in the *Sommer Sentinel*. You were mentioned in the article." She took a scrap of paper and pencil out of her reticule and propped the paper on her lap. "I'm here to interview you."

"I don't recall my name being in the *Sommer Sentinel*." Scofield's brows drew together.

Alicia took the article out of her reticule and handed it to him. He read the piece and stared at her. There was a pensive shimmer in his eyes. After placing the article on his desk, he clasped his hands.

"What could you possibly want from this article?" he casually asked.

"I thought of a pirate at first but decided to change the primary focus of the story to a particular smuggler and his encounter with a villager who will not be coerced." That was as far as she had gotten, but it sounded good once she gave the plot voice.

"And the villager is a woman of integrity."

She nodded.

"Of course she is. And this smuggler, this gentleman of sorts, woos her, and she succumbs to him."

She didn't like the way he gloated, but he *had* come up with a good idea. "Of course not. The woman of integrity—"

"You're not going to tell me that she will rescue and save the smuggler from his evil ways." Scofield was leaning across the desk as if he were trying a case in court. She leaned toward him.

"She deduces his appearances are deceiving. Yes, she tries to save him but not because he is a smuggler. That is how he appears on the outside. Our hero is a spy for England. She will help him to get his message to the King."

The judge drew back, his elbows on the arms of his chair, his fingers tented in front of him as his face broke in a wide smile.

"You moved from the romance of a pirate to that of a spy. I have found that pirates and spies alike are not comely looking men. As for your woman of integrity, people want something for nothing and with the war, there is a shortage of able-bodied men. Mix in an element of corruption and you have spies and smugglers prospering... and villagers, some with a great deal of integrity, needing money. They will do anything to clothe and feed their family."

"But you can make them testify." She added a tone of indignation to her voice and hoped she sounded outraged.

"The smugglers are resourceful. If no one witnesses them commit their crime, no one can point their finger. The smugglers insist the villagers turn away so they will claim truthfully they saw nothing."

"What about shipwrecks? The smuggler may control the villagers, but what about the sailors? Surely, they can't control them."

"Salvage laws are precise. It is illegal to claim salvage on board a wrecked ship if anyone is alive." He gave her an icy stare that made her raise her hand to her throat. "You're right to be horrified. A shipwreck is a death sentence for any sailor who survives."

Her idea of the adventurous, romantic smuggler-spy hero who finds his lady love was quickly turning villainous.

"I'm not sure you can create a smuggler hero who is worthy of a woman of integrity, but you do have an alternative. Some smugglers attack ships, wreck them, and wait for the cargo to float ashore. Abandoned cargo is common property."

Her mind raced for a story line. She imagined Justin's story would be a dark one with plenty of action and the reality of smuggling and spies. Although… the thought of abandoned cargo could be useful. She stood and smoothed out her pelisse. Scofield stood as well.

"You've given me a great deal of information and much to think about. I appreciate your time." She walked toward the door.

"Lady Alicia. If you have more questions, please come to me. You would be surprised who are smugglers or receive their booty."

Inwardly, Alicia shivered, thinking of Elkington accepting the bottles of brandy from Mr. Perkins.

"You have no idea who is friend or foe."

She needed to alleviate the judge's unease.

"I'm touched by your concern. I will be careful." She turned to leave but hesitated. "And I will seek you out should I have any further questions."

She left Scofield. As she opened the garden gate, she collided into Justin.

"Good day, Lady Alicia." His smile easily spread across his face. He appeared sincerely happy to see her, but was he besotted?

"I received a letter from your uncle today."

His smile faded and put her on alert. He said nothing.

"He informed me he would be arriving in Sommer-by-the-Sea by the end of the week, on his way to Alnwick. But it was something else he mentioned that was curious. He said he tried to tell me something several times and was glad it was resolved. I was certain he meant that part of his note for someone else. Do you have any idea what he is talking about?"

A smile returned to his lips, but it didn't quite reach his eyes. "My uncle wanted to tell you that he was retiring and that I would be taking over the company."

She stared at his chest without saying a word as her anger grew.

Then she said, "You've been aware of this all along, that you would be a competing author as well as my editor and publisher, yet you said nothing." She raised her head.

To his credit, he was as sheepish as a schoolboy who had been reprimanded.

"First you hide that you're J. C. Melrose, and now this. Is your attention, your display of affection to make me stay with Caulfield Publishing?"

The astonished expression on his face faded, replaced by one that made her step back.

But he would have none of that. He stepped closer to her. Close enough that her vision was filled with his face.

"I may be many things, but I don't toy with women to get what I want." His curt voice lashed out at her. "What I have said and done I have done with honesty. Not with duplicity. Neither I nor my uncle will keep you where you don't want to be. You're an intelligent woman. One I respect. I would never…do that."

She wanted to believe him. She wanted him to fight for her, for them as hard as he fought in the war for his men.

That was a fantasy, like her stories.

His actions should be no surprise. Effie had been ridiculous. *Besotted.* He wasn't infatuated with her. Taking over as publisher, he wanted to secure his own business, possibly even stop publishing her stories… even though they created a good deal of income for Caulfield Publishing.

She looked at him for any indication she was wrong but

found no tenderness or passion. No, his cold and proud stare pinned her in place.

Justin was lost to her. Her mind raced to find the words to make this right. There was nothing she could say to quell her doubts or make the situation better.

He hadn't moved. He was fixed in place as she.

Angry, hurt, and confused, she reeled at the simple fact that was clear to her.

She loved him and obviously, he did not love her.

CHAPTER THIRTEEN

JUSTIN STOOD IN front of her. The muscle in his jaw tensed as he struggled to keep his composure. Demanding her full attention, he stepped close. His face inches away from hers. Close enough her breath warmed his cheek. She retreated, but he advanced, determined not to give his quarry an inch.

Out of necessity, he had been many things in his life. Some situations he had faced required him to ignore values that were dear to him.

Some were too sacred to compromise. Relationships were built on loyalty and trust. He would not compromise those. It took this crossroad for him to come face to face with his integrity. His direction was clear, as hurtful as it was for him.

"I'm not sure who desired the intimacy more, you or me. One thing is certain, we both wanted that kiss. That is something neither you nor I can deny."

By all that was holy, he wanted to take her in his arms and kiss away her doubts. Was he going mad?

"If what you say is true, then tell me why you didn't inform me of your good fortune." She then asked in a tone as icy as her stare, "Were you contemplating declining your uncle's offer?"

"I was getting accustomed to the idea." He relaxed his aggressive stance.

Alicia didn't take the opportunity to step back. The small win gave him hope.

"Ah, your books are not published by Caulfield Publishing."

"Caulfield publishes all my books."

She drew her eyebrows together. "When did you make plans to read your book here?"

"I didn't. My uncle made the arrangements. He was aware I was traveling here to see Barrington and asked me to bring the books. The reading was an afterthought. I found out on my way here. Why do you ask?"

"My plans were made last month." She was deep in thought. "He is obviously manipulating us. I'm not sure how involved you are in his dubious plan."

"I have no idea what my uncle is up to or what he would gain. I assure you I am taken back as much as you are."

"I will not be controlled, by anyone. Do you hear?"

"Control you? No," he shook his head. "You misunderstand."

"Do I? I hand in my manuscript. The next time I see my work is when he sends me the published book."

"You reap the benefit of your stories in the sales."

"The only alternative I had was to sell Caulfield Publishing the copyright. I wasn't given the alternative of a consignment or commission agreement. He owns my work."

No wonder she was upset. Her books sold well, and she had gained little other than recognition. A change in her contract wouldn't be difficult.

"For your information, Captain Caulfield," she poked his chest with her index finger, "your esteemed publishing company isn't the only one who wants to publish my books."

He didn't move. He stood as if a drill sergeant was dressing him down.

"Nothing to say. I didn't think so. The William Lane Publishing Company contacted me three weeks ago." She looked away from him. "I've no idea why I hesitated, why I felt loyal to your uncle."

"You've been successful at Caulfield Publishing," he said.

"I've made Caulfield Publishing very successful with my 'little stories.'"

He touched her hand, the one that rubbed the worry stone. She lifted her chin in a sweeping quick motion, causing her to lose several hair pins.

"You're an excellent author. I read your book and listened to the passion in your voice at the reading. So did the others. You held them and told a captivating story in a powerful way. You left everyone, *everyone* speechless. And that wasn't the only time. You were just as passionate and convincing when you told me the stories at the cathedral and dungeon. That is a gift."

"You're surprised that I'm good at my craft?"

"Not at all, but I think you are."

She removed his hand from hers.

He wasn't willing to give up his fight. Not yet.

⋙✦⋘

ALICIA LISTENED AS Captain Caulfield kept speaking. He wasn't going to give up.

Several times she thought to turn, walk away. She didn't. He knew her deepest secret but wasn't speaking about the benefits of Caulfield Publishing. Nor did he detract from William Lane. He asked her what she wanted from her publisher.

She told him she wanted a commission and the right to refuse editorial changes.

"Your requests are reasonable. Have you presented them?"

"There is another issue. William Lane Publishing has more prestige."

"William Lane is larger than Caulfield Publishing. But it doesn't deal in your type of stories," he said.

"My type of stories?" That perked her attention.

"Examine what he publishes and how he manages stories like yours. Speak to those authors. They can give you the insight you need to make your decision."

She was surprised at the approach he was taking. He was counseling her on how to make her decision, not telling her or even trying to convince her to stay with Caulfield.

What he said made sense. She needed time to work this out. Staying with Caulfield and working with him, would be... No. Now wasn't the time to dream. This had to be a business decision and not an emotional one.

"Effie gave us a challenge," she said.

"Yes, she did. I'm... missing how that has anything to do with our discussion."

"If my story is the better one, I'll accept William Lane's offer. If it is not..." She wasn't about to say anything about losing. "I will remain at Caulfield."

"You're going to base your writing career on one short story?" He stood with his mouth gaping open.

"I don't plan to lose." She let her words hang in the air. "If you will excuse me. I have some thinking and planning to do. I appreciate your concern."

He bent close to her before she left.

"I accept your challenge. A man would spit in his palm and shake on the deal. I'll spare you. In its place I'll say, may the best story win."

She removed her glove.

"This will have to do." She shook his hand hard, once. "May the best writer win." She was off.

HE RAKED HIS hand through his hair and let out a deep breath.

Now what?

If the situation wasn't dire, he'd laugh. Caulfield Publishing may have lost its premier author due to him and he hadn't yet started his new position.

He glanced in her direction and made out a lone figure in

robin's egg blue traipsing along the cliff not far from the beach path.

Alicia's desire to control her own destiny was not unreasonable even if her demands were a bit foreign to him.

In the service, control was out of your hands. There were times he had to deal with orders that were ill-conceived. Those were the times his own resourcefulness and those of his men kept them alive. He ached for control. To get it, he worked hard, rose through the ranks.

Alicia was fighting the same battle, and he admired her for it.

"By all that is holy," he murmured in frustration. "This is a mess."

He had no idea she was the other author Lane was considering. He would decline the offer in a heartbeat if it would make things right.

He too, had gotten post. One letter was from his uncle announcing he would be in Sommer-by-the-Sea. The other message was a brief note from William Lane.

"The characters in the other author's stories seek their personal happiness by departing from the well-established restrictions of our social order. This is totally improbable and not the type of story William Lane Publishing wishes to promote. The author is no longer under consideration. Your stories tell of the trials and tribulations of our military and elevate the pride of the British Empire. We'd be pleased to publish and promote your stories, if you so desired."

Lane's reasoning was flawed. If he had been at the library, listened to her read, witnessed how her audience was spellbound, he would have had her sign a contract then and there.

Justin glanced at the cliff. She was gone.

Go after her.

Why? What more could he say?

He made his way to the market square and on toward Sommer Chase, his mission clear. Write to William Lane, thank him for his consideration, and decline the offer.

His spirit should be lighter and his prospects positive with the weight of the decision gone. It wasn't. He could face his uncle's reaction to losing his best author but had no joy in Alicia finding out her much sought-after ascent to a prestigious publisher was dashed. And he could do nothing to prevent or console her.

Perhaps he should tell her Caulfield was disappointed with her decision, and should she change her mind they would gladly resume publishing her stories.

The idea faded as quickly as he brought it to the surface. Once she found out he had been given the offer, she would think his words were insulting.

To have the prize in hand only to have it slip away was more devastating than never having had the prize at all.

Alicia was his prize. He shut his eyes, trying to force her out of his mind, and realized she was permanently fixed there.

"To have the prize," he mumbled, unable to finish the sentence.

CHAPTER FOURTEEN

ALICIA MARCHED DOWN the path to the beach. The breeze whipped at her skirt, pushing her along.

"How did I not see through his veneer?" She kicked a small rock out of her way and kept moving.

Halfway down the path, the wind shifted. She took a deep breath and came to an abrupt halt. Lavender and citrus. Controlling the smile that threatened to bloom, she pivoted, ready to continue their discussion.

No one was there. She swallowed around a hot lump in her throat and glanced at the crest of the cliff. He may still be where she left him. Surely, they could work this out.

No! the little voice deep inside her screamed in rebellion. He was no different than any other man.

Putting one foot in front of the other, she continued on to the beach, plodding along at a steady cadence along the surf. The crash of the waves and renewed rawness of the wind mirrored her turmoil. Try as she might to rid herself of Captain Caulfield, he was part of her.

The bend in the beach behind her, the rockslide to the cave was up ahead. Alicia climbed up the slide to prevent her skirt from getting wet from the surf creeping up the beach. She stood and looked out at the sea.

The wind, more forceful now, tugged at her skirt and pelisse.

She didn't care if she lost every hairpin. The briny air was invigorating. The roar of the sea and the waves were calming. The untamed power was what she loved about the beach. It loosened her mind.

Men and their control. No one thought her writing would come to anything. Her mother and sister encouraged her, but her father? He was a dear and she loved him, but he did not understand her need to flourish on her own merits.

Be like your sister, he'd say. Beatrice had a stubborn streak and pouted to get her way with Elkington. Alicia didn't want to cajole a man nor barter with him to get what she deserved. She wanted a strong man, who was loyal, true, and sensitive, who listened. A man like… Justin Caulfield.

Was he the man she wanted?

She screamed into the wind. That small little voice may be telling her one thing, but her heart said something different.

How could she still feel strongly about him after his deception?

And Effie? *This silly challenge.* Why did she make this bargain with him? Even if she wanted to, going back on her word was not an option. No, not now.

She'd make this the best story she ever wrote. Mr. Anonymous would have to think twice about her work and William Lane would beg her to leave Caulfield.

Then there was Mrs. Bainbridge. Could she be right? Lane Publishing might be no better than where she was now. If she stayed with Caulfield, she might be able to negotiate with Justin for some control of her work.

After all, her books performed well and working with Justin would be… nice.

Alicia held her pendant, closed her eyes. Tendrils of hair whipped in the wind. Waves pounded on the shore setting off loose sprays of water while they washed over the sand and rocks. The crashing roar echoed in her ears until it blocked out that little voice and Justin Caulfield.

"Some smugglers may appear to be gentlemen, but I assure you they are ruthless" … "A shipwreck is a death sentence for any sailor" … "Your hero is not worthy of your Olivia."

Several minutes later, she opened her eyes, ready to focus. She let her imagination go.

The raging storm pulled the struggling ship toward the rocky shore. On the rockslide that reached out into the water, a horse stood tethered with a lit lantern that glowed as a beacon into the moonless night.

Olivia stood on the cliff, unable to move. The ship was close now, heaving and tossing with each rising wave. It dipped low in the water then rose with the swell. It seemed to hover at the crest of the wave for a heartbeat, maybe two, then plummeted, crashing onto the rocks with a final, terrible squeal of breaking timber.

Men on shore manned small boats that lined the beach and took to the sea. They fought the angry surf and made their way to their quarry. Like insects, they crept up the sides of the dying ship.

Moments later, her brows drew together as sailors' cries for mercy reached her ears.

The situation wasn't much better on the beach. The sand was littered with splintered wood. Part of the broken mast was wedged in the rocks, torn sails hanging from its yardarm. Cargo crates washed up on shore, along with the odds and ends of personal belongings.

Men pulled themselves out of the angry surf and clawed their way onto the shore. That was where the melee was worse. Swarms of men brandishing swords and knives came down on the survivors like a pack of angry wolves. One by one the brave sailors fought for their lives.

Those not killing survivors dragged the crates and barrels to safety as the fight went on. They had no time to secure their booty. In the distance at the foot of the cliff, men moved fast and stowed their plunder. The tide was coming in quickly now. This part of the beach would soon be under water.

Alicia opened her eyes and squinted at the sun. A satisfied smile spread across her face. The story emerged nicely.

She glanced over her shoulder at the cave. It was the perfect place to hide plunder, a good setting for a short story.

It was at least two hours before high tide, plenty of time for her to investigate the cave and get back up the cliff. She needed to be in the cave, smell, feel, touch it to finish her tale.

She walked toward the cave, navigating the slick rocks. Of the several caves that dotted the foot of the cliff, she veered to the one she hid in all those years ago. The one she had shared with Justin.

CHAPTER FIFTEEN

THE CLASH OF metal on metal, flesh hitting flesh, along with grunts and groans filled the exercise room at Sommer Chase.

Peter and Simon fenced at one end of the room while Barrington and Justin sparred at the other.

Barrington let loose a right jab and caught Justin in the stomach, winding him.

"Tighten that mid-section. You're vulnerable if you don't. Now, again."

Justin, his head tucked and his fists protecting his face, glared at Barrington as he jabbed with his left. Barrington ducked the next punch. Justin was ready for him.

He shifted his weight to his right as his friend ducked. He put all his power behind a right upper cut and clipped Barrington's jaw.

Barrington, now back against the wall, raised his hand. "Hold." He wiggled his jaw.

"We've been at this now for an hour. You're ruthless today. You're after me as if your life depends upon it."

Justin said nothing. He stood with his fists up ready to continue the fight.

"I need a rest, and so do you before you kill me and yourself. I haven't seen you this...determined to kill someone since we left the Continent.

"Take this. You need to cool off." Barrington handed him a cool wet cloth.

Justin lowered his fists. He shook his head, sending a spray of sweat everywhere, then wiped his face and the back of his neck.

His friend stood and waited for him to say something.

"I've gotten myself into an awkward situation, one that I can see no way of escaping."

Barrington remained silent. He was not going to make this easy for him. He might as well get this over with.

"Alicia—"

"I thought so," he interrupted.

Justin glared at him and continued.

"As I was saying, Alicia was not aware I was an author, especially not J. C. Melrose. My name was associated with hers in a recent review to which she did not take kindly."

"Why didn't you speak up?"

He rubbed the towel in his hair and looked at his friend.

"It wasn't from the lack of trying. That doesn't matter. It didn't take me long to realize she didn't think kindly of J. C. Melrose. I didn't want that to be in the way of our getting better acquainted."

"That didn't work out well," Barrington said.

"No. It did not. When I did tell her, she jumped to the conclusion that I lied to her. That I neglected to inform her of whom I was in order to humiliate her at the reading." He hung the towel around his neck. "That is the *last* thing I wanted. I managed to smooth that over."

"I don't understand. Why are you upset?"

"She got a letter from Uncle Isaac alluding to some change at the company."

Barrington grabbed him by both shoulders. "You didn't *tell* her you were taking over the publishing company?"

"He tried to tell her, and I didn't find the right time until she…"

"Cornered you?"

He nodded.

"I would laugh if it wasn't so sad." Barrington dropped his hands and shook his head.

"There's more. She received a letter from William Lane Publishing. They wanted to speak to her about publishing her stories."

"Now you're concerned you'll lose your star author."

"And this challenge."

"The writing challenge that Lady Euphemia mentioned?"

"Yes. Alicia has increased the prize. If her story is judged to be the best, she will leave and go to the other publisher. If mine is, she will stay where she is. Except…"

He stood like a young boy who filched a tart from the cooling rack in the kitchen.

"I *also* received a letter from William Lane. They are no longer considering Alicia. They offered me the position. While the offer is tempting, I'm not interested in the position. I have yet to tell them."

"That is a problem. If she goes to the other publisher, she will find they are no longer interested in her work… leaving her without *any* publisher." Barrington shook his head.

"No, but her books sell well. If she wanted, she could publish them herself." Justin pulled the towel from his neck and threw it into a basket. "Not my first day at my job and I've cost the company its best author." He looked at Barrington. "I love her," he murmured.

"I'm well aware how you feel for her. The question is what do you plan to do about it?"

"*Do* about it? What can I do about it? Visit her at her home for tea and say, 'Please, forgive me, for being…an arse.'"

"Why not. You've done it before under worse conditions. You sought me out the night before a battle to settle a disagreement between us. Or did you do that for me so if you died on the battlefield, you could go knowing all was forgiven?"

Justin stared at him in disbelief. When the man's face broke into a wide smile, he laughed along with him.

"You're right. Admitting I could have handled this better could not be as bad as it was confessing to you, but…" he looked at his friend, hoping he understood, "I hurt her and that tears at my heart. She may never forgive me."

"You won't know until you ask her for forgiveness. The thought is usually worse than what actually happens."

"That's what you told me the first time I spoke to a soldier's family."

"I didn't say speaking to the families would be easy. I knew you were the best man for that assignment, my most compassionate man for that detail. I also knew you had the strength to complete the task. Just as you do now. I have no idea if she will forgive you, but you will know you did everything to make it right. So will she."

Barrington handed him his jacket.

"I also have to tell Isaac that we have lost our best author," he said as he shrugged into it.

"You're so sure she will take her book someplace else. Wait until she tells you. Alicia may surprise you. As for the best author, what is wrong with your stories? I like them."

"My stories are—"

"Reese, forgive my intrusion."

They both spun around as an agitated Honoria Bainbridge rushed into the room.

"Halt!" Peter called. Simon withdrew his sword. Both men went to Barrington's side.

"Honoria?" Barrington said.

Mrs. Bainbridge, along with Effie and Lady Elkington, hurried into the room, worried expressions on their faces.

Justin was halfway across the room. "What's happened?"

"She didn't come back to the manor," Lady Elkington said.

"Nor did she come to tea with me," Mrs. Bainbridge told Barrington. "It isn't like her to miss an appointment with

Honoria." Mrs. Bainbridge twisted the linen in her hand. Justin was not surprised when Barrington removed the linen from her hand, wiped her eyes, and took her in his arms.

"I expected Alicia two hours ago," Honoria said, looking up into Barrington's eyes. "The longer I waited the more concerned I grew. It is not like her to not send me a message. I went to Hartmore Manor to inquire."

"I'm sure she is fine. I was with her earlier today." Justin said the words, but he knew something was wrong as soon as they were out of his mouth.

"She's been so involved in her research," Lady Elkington said.

"Research? What research?" Justin asked.

"I met her at the inn for an early tea," Effie said. "She was doing research for the short story and interviewed people."

"I'm concerned, Reese," Honoria said.

"Who did she interview?" Justin glanced at Barrington, Peter, and Simon. His concern was mirrored on their faces. Peter and Simon put their weapons away.

"Mr. Hawkins walked into the inn with her," Effie said. "She wanted more information to write her story. She asked him, but he had nothing to add to what he wrote in his editorial. We both read through his article and found people for her to speak to. We were fortunate. Mr. Perkins was in the inn and Commander Terrell arrived while she was speaking to him. She interviewed them both. When I left her, she was on her way to interview Judge Scofield."

"Did you say Commander Terrell, Commander *Matthew* Terrell?" Justin asked.

"Yes." Effie stared at him.

"We were introduced to him the beginning of September in London," Lady Elkington said. "Have you met the commander?"

Justin's heart raced as raw anger shot through him. "Yes. I was with Matthew Terrell when he died in Salamanca two years ago."

Lady Elkington gasped. "That can't be."

Mrs. Bainbridge stepped away from Barrington and went to Lady Elkington.

"Come, Beatrice, sit down," Mrs. Bainbridge said.

"If he's not Commander Terrell, who is he?" Lady Elkington stared at Mrs. Bainbridge as she helped her to a chair.

Justin knew *exactly* who was posing as Matthew Terrell. He turned to Barrington and didn't miss his silent signal to Peter and Simon.

"What haven't you told me?" he asked.

"I've been working with the Custom Service and Land Guard ferreting out rumors." Barrington nodded to Peter and Simon. "We need to bring the Guard here."

The men left wordlessly.

Barrington turned to the others.

"This puzzle has many pieces, and we are trying to fit them together. We're considering a connection between the stolen Walmer gold in Kent and the smugglers in the village. With the larger ports closely watched by the Land Guard, a small village like ours provided the best way for them to move the gold out of the country."

"Why out of the country?" Effie asked.

"Some people would smuggle English gold out of the country and bring it to France for Napoleon. He still has support from French Nationalists," Barrington said.

"What has Alicia gotten herself into?" Effie asked.

"Where else did she go?" Barrington asked.

"I spoke to her when she was leaving the judge's office. That didn't go well," Justin said. He stopped his hand from raking through his hair. "She wanted time to think. I offered to escort her, but she would have none of that."

"Alicia does her thinking on the beach," Honoria said.

"When I last saw her, she was walking along the cliff," he said. "I shouldn't have let her go alone."

"Alicia can walk the path and the beach blindfolded," Effie said.

Lady Ellington jumped to her feet, and her wild eyes flicked from one person to the other.

"What if she's tumbled? The cave. Or if she went inside and fell asleep…" She looked from one face to the other. "The tide."

"I know where the cave is," Justin said. "I will bring her back to you, safely."

Lady Elkington grabbed his arm as he tried to leave.

"Who is Commander Terrell?" she asked.

"I have my suspicions." He put his hand over hers. "I will bring her back to you. I promise."

Yes, he had his suspicions, and hoped to God he was wrong. Without another word, he hurried out the door.

CHAPTER SIXTEEN

ALICIA, SLOWED BY the rubble of stones and slick seaweed, trudged around the boulders and up the rock incline to the cave.

She didn't stop to catch her breath until she reached the entrance. With the churning surf in the background, she stopped and stared into the dark abyss. Her mind reliving the panicked memories of years ago.

A few minutes was all she needed. Smell, touch, observe. If Justin managed to move beyond his fear, so could she. Grabbing her courage, she stepped inside.

The cave was deadly quiet. Huge flat rocks littered the floor like an ancient mosaic pattern. There was no time to linger. There was one place in the cave that frightened her the most. That was where she needed to go, to the edge of the darkness, the tenth boulder that stood guard in front of the deep pool. Then she could leave.

The roar of the crashing waves echoed in the large empty space. She ran her hand over the boulders for the secret directions.

The first three weren't difficult. The next mark was faint, eroded by the abrasive water and sand. She went on from stone to stone, avoiding the debris.

The fifth mark was missing. Had she mis-stepped? No. She

trusted her intuition. This stone was correct.

She hesitated for a moment. The next three would lead in a straight line. She needed to find the right one, and in the weak light the stones were difficult to make out.

Trusting her intuition, she walked to the left and was relieved to feel the mark of the sixth stone. She quickly found seven and eight.

She peered into the darkness. Only two other large boulders remained.

In the depths of the damp cave and with the hypnotic beat of the waves, the sound of old chains rattled in the pool beyond. She closed her eyes.

The villagers lined up along the beach not far from the foot of the cliff, their backs toward the beach. The sounds of men dying rang out above the pounding surf. Olivia Fitzwilliam melted back toward the cliff. Thankful there was no moonlight, she went unseen as she scurried behind the rocks. She must act before more innocent men died. Careful not to be observed, she slipped into the cave.

Olivia knew the cave well and went deep inside. Her eyes were of little use here. Guided along by the old scratches she and her sister put on the rocks from the games they played, she continued on to the tenth and last boulder.

Her hands ran along the wall for the crates she and Louise stowed earlier in the day. They were stuffed with every knife and weapon they could find. Reluctantly, she added her father's throwing knife into the mix, the one she practiced with. His weapon was her contribution.

She was sure she was in the correct spot but found nothing. Odd. She must be turned around in the darkness.

"Are you looking for this?"

Olivia spun at the sound of a man's voice, Matthew Terrell. She flinched as a light flared but forced herself to remain calm as her eyes adjusted to the brightness.

The French smuggler turned spy held her father's knife. She was angered, but that wasn't what surprised her. It was Louise standing next to him that did.

She glared at her friend and didn't hide her disappointment and fury.

"Don't... don't, glare at me that way." Louise shifted from one foot to the other.

"Why not? You should not be surprised at my reaction. That you dishonor your brother – who this man killed – when all your brother did was try to protect you and his livelihood. You stand with a man who—"

"Who will protect me!"

"For only as long as he needs you. Listen to me, Louise." She paused. Above the echoing surf were the screams of men dying. "Do you hear that? They're dying. He told those men, the sailors on his ship, that he would protect them, too."

She said nothing and let Louise consider her words.

"Don't listen to her. I'll take care of you like I said." Matthew puffed up his chest. His menacing stance didn't intimidate her. There was too much at stake. She had to warn Hugh that the villagers may not stand as one.

"Yes, like you protected Louise's brother." She glanced at Louise. A shadow of doubt clouded her face.

Unease crept into the man's expression.

"How did you protect him? With a sword or a knife in his back?" Olivia asked.

"That's not true," Louise said as she faced Matthew. "You said you loved me."

"Oh, Louise. Look at his face," Olivia said. "The lie is written plainly for you to see."

Louise took a hesitant step to the side and stared at Matthew.

His smug expression gave him away.

"What have I done?" Louise murmured and ran from the cave.

"Aren't you going to stop her?" Olivia asked.

"Why? She would have learned the truth soon enough. She served her purpose. The others will take care of her." Relaxed, the man laughed. "You have been a thorn in my side, putting doubt in the villagers' minds. I regret I will have to make an example of you."

"I wouldn't try if I were you." From behind Matthew came a voice, the timber of which no one would forget. It was deep, male. With a quality that made people tremble.

Olivia stared into the burning eyes of Hugh Talbot.

Terrell spun around and was met with three quick left jabs. Each one snapped his head back. The man did not fall. The smuggler ducked rather than take another punch, but Hugh was ready. He led with his right hip and a mighty right upper cut exploded, sending the smuggler to the ground.

Olivia moved to the side to give them room when all of a sudden—

"Ouch." Alicia bent down to rub her toe and was startled to find a glistening stone. She picked it up, brushed off the sand, and examined it closely. A coin of some sort. She ran her finger over it and felt the engraving but was unable to make out what it was.

She bent down to see if there were more and came face to face with something hard that didn't belong in the cave. She removed glops of sand from its top and found a wooden crate.

Alicia nudged the crate and wasn't surprised when it didn't move. Had she found the French brandy? She stuffed the coin into her reticule, put her little bag down and began to remove the sand from the top of the crate. Slowly, an image emerged. It wasn't marked on the crate, but rather on material draped over the box. As she removed more sand, she made out three golden lions on a red background joined to the stern section of three gold ships on a blue background. She sat back on her heels. This was the flag of the Cinque Port in Kent.

The shock of discovery hit her full force. Hesitating, she bit her lip not sure how to proceed. But the mystery of what was under the flag won out. She pulled the flag off to find the lid in pieces. Beneath the splintered wood were bags. Several were empty, but the ones underneath were full. She lifted one and heard the jingling of coins. This had to be the missing Walmer gold.

What was it doing here?

Judge Scofield had to be told. A king's ransom would be tempting to anyone. She stood, brushed herself off, ready to leave.

What if someone removed the gold before the judge arrived?

A smile slowly spread across her face. She searched anxiously for a place to hide the gold. Finally, she glanced behind her, at the ninth boulder, the one she hid behind all those years ago. There was plenty of room for the bags and no one would find them in the dark.

One by one she pulled the bags out of the crate and stashed them out of sight. Once she was done, she gathered rocks of a similar weight, filled the crate, and replaced the empty bags as well.

Done at last, she scattered the splintered wood on top and put the flag in place. She was replacing the sand when a small surge of water surrounded the crate.

Sheer fright raced through her as she looked toward the entrance. The tide. How long had she been here? She had to leave.

"This is a good hiding place." Alicia jumped at the sound of the man's voice echoing in the cavern.

"Yes, everyone is looking near Kent. No one will search this far north," a younger man said.

She couldn't let the thieves find her. She spun, trying to find a place to hide. There was no room behind the boulder with the gold. She'd have to go deeper into the cave to the edge of darkness. To the tenth boulder. It was the only place left for her to hide.

The voices came closer.

Without another thought, she scurried up the incline and sat behind the rock. She pulled her skirt close to keep it out of sight. If they left now, there was a good chance of leaving before the men found her.

"Not that way. Up this way," a younger man said.

The voices were familiar, but they were out of place and distorted by the echo. She couldn't identify them.

"Behind that boulder," the younger man said.

As she glanced at the crate from her hiding place, she caught a glimpse of her blue reticule on the ground partially covered with sand. There was no time to retrieve it and return to her hiding place. She prayed her little bag would go unnoticed.

Another surge of water, more forceful than the last spread across the ground. Her reticule was loosened from the sand and pushed toward her.

She reached for her little bag. Her fingers brushed the material, but it remained outside her grasp. Another surge. Once again, she stretched as far as possible, but it was pulled away before she could snatch it. She watched in horror as it floated and bobbed in the water not far from the men. She prayed they didn't notice the patch of blue material. A larger surge came around the boulder, captured the reticule and drew it out toward the sea.

Relieved, she slumped against the rock. But that didn't last long. The two men were between her and freedom. With the tide advancing, the men didn't want to be here any more than she did. All she could do was wait, be patient, and ready to act when the opportunity arose.

The men kept talking. She couldn't make out what they were saying. They must know the tide is rising and would fill up the cave. The panic of years ago came flooding back. She had to leave. The water wasn't about to wait for them to finish their conversation. Still they didn't move. Did they plan to swim out of here?

Stay calm.

"It's under the flag," the older man said. "Where's James?"

"He's your man, not mine. My men follow my orders without question. I haven't been here before, but I will keep this place in mind for the future. There are many things you can hide in here and no one will ever find them," the younger man said.

Alicia's brows came together as she tried again to place who the men were. Even with the echo and roar of the water she knew those voices.

She peeked around the boulder as the men pulled the flag off the crate.

"I told you the gold was here. Now, we must leave," the older man continued.

Alicia's eyes widened.

"I'll have my men bring you the brandy. Help me get this out," the younger man said.

"Are you out of your mind? We can't lift this by ourselves. Leave it here. This cave is underwater at high tide. The crate and its contents aren't going anywhere, I assure you."

Alicia pressed her back against the boulder, her anger building, and a sinking feeling turning her stomach. She knew who both men were.

JUSTIN RACED DOWN the cliff path, unconcerned he was ill-dressed for the cold. The surf was turbulent. The sea was advancing. An occasional wave reached the face of the cliff.

He hurried off the path and dashed along the beach, kicking up sprays of water in a desperate effort to reach the cave.

With each wave the water advanced. He didn't have much time.

Justin turned at the sharp bend and stopped. Winded, he bent over with his hands on his thighs, catching his breath. He lifted his head and glanced up the coastline. All he saw was water and the white caps of the tidal waves as they took over the beach.

There was no way for her to reach the path without getting soaked. She was smart enough not to stay inside the cave. Wasn't she? Did she panic? Was she unable to move?

Why did she have to come here, at this time of day? She was aware of the dangers. Hadn't she learned her lesson?

He wanted to thrash some sense into her, but more than that he wanted her to be safe.

Justin hurried on ahead. Slowed by the incoming tide, he forced his heavy feet to move faster. He glanced at the cliff face and there, up ahead saw the entrance to the cave.

He pressed on until he was about ten yards from the opening.

No one was there. He wasn't sure if he was relieved or concerned. Where was the woman?

Water flowed out of the cave. Annoyed and frustrated, there was nothing for him to do. It would be just like her to be sitting with Mrs. Bainbridge or back at Hartmore Manor sipping tea while he was soaked to the bone.

He glanced at the opening. Was she inside? Injured? He headed toward the entrance and stopped. Caught in the steady stream of backwash coming out of the cave was a robin's egg blue reticule, Alicia's little bag. She'd never leave it behind.

He hurried to snatch her bag before the surf took it into the sea. He opened the string and took out the wet article, a pencil, a piece of foolscap, and a gold coin. Yes, this was hers.

He examined the coin and saw the laurel circle with the initials *TLS*. He looked at the cave opening and knew she was in danger.

He stuffed the little bag into his waistband and hiked up to the cave entrance. With each step he was determined he would either scold her for her foolishness, or kiss her thoroughly, thankful she was safe.

CHAPTER SEVENTEEN

ALICIA'S STOMACH ROILED a warning as she pressed her back against the cool boulder trying to ward off the nausea. Judge Scofield. She had known him all her life. How could he?

Matthew Terrell. A smuggler? A killer? That was more fitting than an acting governor or eligible bachelor. A building anger replaced her unsettled stomach.

"Our job is almost done. You should be very happy, my friend. You have made an excellent deal and have fine French brandy, and your life. I promised you I would take care of you."

The tinge of excitement in Terrell's voice almost made her smile. Wait until they opened their treasure chest and looked inside.

A surge of water ran along the floor and up the small incline where she hid. She pulled her pelisse closer. Her hem was already wet.

"This crate won't budge." Terrell's irritated voice echoed. "You may be correct. Low tide will be easier."

The water, deeper now, swirled on the floor creating small eddies. Once again, the heavy wool slipped from her grasp and floated past the boulder. As quietly as she could, she retrieved the soaked material.

"Now, come along before we have to swim out of here."

The judge's voice was halfway between a whisper and a

shout. It was deep and rumbling like the crash of the sea around them, but full of a panic she had never heard from him before.

The water sloshed and she imagined the men walking out of the cave. Thank goodness they were leaving. Even though the water kept rising, she would wait a bit longer until she was sure they were gone before she got to her feet.

Silence. A metallic sound caught her attention. The old chains. Satisfied the men were gone, Alicia stood, stepped around the boulder, and stopped.

Alicia faced the judge and Terrell.

"Shall we go?" She tried to conceal her fear and swallowed around the tight knot in her throat. Seizing all the courage she had, she started for the cave opening.

The commander grabbed her arm and pulled her back.

"Release me at once," she said in a tense, clipped voice that forbade any further argument.

Her tact succeeded to a point. The commander paused.

"Terrell, I'll take Lady Alicia." The judged moved toward her, but the commander pulled her out of the judge's reach.

"Mon dieu!" Terrell muttered under his breath. "Lady Alicia is not going anywhere."

He turned her to face him. She could see his mind working, trying to decide his next action.

She needed to get out of the cave. At least on the beach she had a chance to get away. The rockslide at the entrance was treacherous with the incoming tide. If she could make her way to the entrance—

"It is unfortunate, but she will not leave here, alive."

"You. Would. Not. Dare." She pushed him away.

The commander slapped her, hard. She rushed at him, but the judge pulled her back. She turned toward Terrel and stared at the point of his knife.

In one fluid move, Terrell grabbed her arm, twisted it behind her back, and held the knife at her throat.

"Don't give me a reason to be any angrier with you than I

am. It will not go well for you," the commander said, his lips close to her ear.

The point of his knife caught the chain of her pendant. With a quick flick of his wrist, he tore it from her neck and pitched it into the darkness.

"A clue of where you've been. Perhaps someone will find it, perhaps not. Qui vivra verra."

A sudden chill hung on the edge of his words. His eyes were ablaze with anger when he bent close to her.

"You should have taken heed to my warning."

CHAPTER EIGHTEEN

J USTIN ENTERED THE cave, the tide waters surged at his feet.

"Terrell, I'll take Lady Alicia."

"Mon dieu! Lady Alicia is not going anywhere. It is unfortunate, but she will not leave here, alive."

Blood pounded in his ear. That voice. Perspiration beaded on his brow. The crashing waves of the unsettled ocean were no better than the explosions of guns and cannons. He was back on the battlefield. Images of the French commander determined to torture and kill every Englishman, especially those Justin commanded flashed through his mind. He had been one of the more fortunate ones.

"You. Would. Not. Dare." Alicia threw the words at the man like sharp knives.

Justin froze. Her tone was the same as when she read at the library. She was unafraid, menacing, and possessed the quality of a wild animal ready to strike.

The sound of a sharp slap echoed through the cave above the sound of rushing water.

Justin's anger became a scalding fury, but he held himself back from rushing to her side. He stepped into the cave with his back against the wall and inched along as quiet as possible. Alicia's life depended upon it.

"Don't give me a reason to be any angrier with you than I

am. It will not go well for you. A clue of where you've been. Perhaps someone will find it, perhaps not. Qui vivra verra. You should have listened to my warning," the Frenchman said.

The Frenchman was the embodiment of the malicious scoundrel he had crafted for his books. Captain Mallory went from story to story following the villain to bring him to justice. The time had come for Justin to put an end to the devil.

The man had terrorized enough people, leaving them broken or dead. Alicia would not be his next victim.

Every location had its advantages and disadvantages, even this one. A quick survey of the area with a military leader's eye and he noted where he had opportunities and identified the obstacles. There was an abundance of hindrances, which just meant he had to work harder to make his opportunities work for him.

That was one of his strengths.

Justin eased along the wall, keeping to the shadows, and thankful the sound of the surging water muffled his progress.

He came around a boulder and in the dim afternoon light made out three people: Alicia, Scofield, and the Frenchman.

The killer's back was to him. After years of this masked man in his head, he wanted to see the man's face.

Alicia stood six feet from him, glaring at the man. A raised red mark brightened her right cheek.

She held herself proud and unflinching. Even bedraggled and soaked, she was regal, determined, and not about to be cowed. She wouldn't give the Frenchman an easy time.

Content she was not in imminent danger, he turned his attention to the judge.

"You will not touch her. Do you understand." The judge's tone made the Frenchman pause. "You do, and you will be explaining to Napoleon why you return to him without his gold."

Justin shifted his attention back to the Frenchman. The ruthlessness and inhumanity of the man symbolized everything he fought against. He wanted to tear the man apart, but with the knife at Alicia's throat, he dared not take any action. The Frenchman did not fear Scofield or Alicia. But the man had every reason to fear *him*.

For years Justin hunted for him, but the Frenchman remained one step ahead. Masquerading as Matthew Terrell was Justin's breaking point. He intended to put an end to the Frenchman and his fiendish games.

Matthew Terrell was not only a hero – Matthew was also his cousin and closest friend since childhood. They did everything together, including go to war. Justin wasn't about to let this fiend drag the man's reputation through the mud.

The water was quickly filling the cave. He had no idea how much time they had before it was completely engulfed. He discounted one idea after another. Even with the judge's brave words, the Frenchmen had no intention of letting Alicia or Scofield live.

A wave slapped against the outside of the cave sending a rush of water inside. Time was slipping away.

"Judge. Your eyes give you away. You're more than happy to pronounce a death sentence but you don't have the stomach to carry out the execution. This won't be as hard as you imagine. Lady Alicia will slip, fall, and be knocked unconscious. With the tide filling the cave, the poor girl will drown, a terrible accident for certain."

Alicia did not react. Justin was grateful for that. No matter what happened, he counted on her to keep her wits.

"Lady Alicia, your family and friends will be worried. You will put them through such torture. Tsk, tsk, tsk." The French-man grabbed her hair and twisted it until she turned toward him. He shook his head, a false sad expression on his face, and let out a deep breath. "It will take days, maybe months before anyone finds you. And all because you refused to take my advice."

Justin's muscles quivered from holding them tense. *A bit longer. Hold on.*

"We can't stay here in the shadows. Up a bit more. I want

you to see me clearly." The Frenchman leaned close to her ear. "Perhaps I will daze you first. I prefer women who are cooperative."

He moved her forward, the knife at her throat.

The Frenchman's tactic was mental torture before physical pain. But he underestimated Lady Alicia Hartley. She was a formidable opponent.

"I said I would take care of her. Give her to me," the judge shouted.

"No. But I don't want to damage her pretty face any more than I must." The Frenchman's voice was deadly serious. "Find me a piece of rope. We will tie her to one of the rocks. If she survives the tide, she will go free. Like your famous witch trials. Qui vivra verra. It won't matter. I will be long gone."

A bit longer, Alicia. I promise he will pay.

The Frenchman would end his game soon. Justin watched and waited ready to strike.

Water swept against the threesome and pushed Alicia off balance. A trickle of blood ran down her neck from the prick of the knife.

Justin, stoic and intense, waited. The Frenchman used his blades with the precision of a surgeon. The man made him stand by and observe when he sliced into his soldiers, torturing them.

It was only Barrington's arrival that saved him from a similar fate.

Alicia shifted in the water, getting her footing. She stared off as if in another world. That was when her eyes found him. Justin gave her a nod of encouragement and hoped she understood.

"You don't have anything to say, Lady Alicia? No last words?"

The judge grabbed for the knife, but the Frenchman was prepared. A quick flick of the blade and Scofield howled in pain. Blood drenched his chest.

Justin took advantage of the diversion. In two steps, he freed her from the villain's grasp and pulled her behind him, eager to at last put a face to this man.

The Frenchman turned and stared at him.

"Captain Caulfield. So, we meet again, and so soon."

"Mr. Pratt," Justin said smoothly with no expression. "I can't say it's a pleasure to see you again."

"Again?" Scofield asked.

"Mr. Pratt and I shared the mail coach from London to Harrogate."

"Always gracious. Your reputation precedes you. You remain a legend on the Continent. The ruthless Highlander. There are many Frenchmen who would like to be in my place, in front of you with a blade…with you unarmed."

"You call that little pick a blade? It was always your preferred weapon. It became quite evident that you had no skill with anything else."

Pratt's eyes widened.

Justin had to keep Pratt's focus on him. "You're not frightening an old man or a young woman." He advanced. Water rushed into the cave halfway up his legs. He needed to distract the man. Move him away from Alicia and Scofield.

"Scofield, take Alicia out of here," Justin said. His eyes didn't leave Pratt.

"Scofield?" Pratt glanced between the judge and Justin before he stepped back to avoid being caught between the two. "I should have known."

"I will not leave." Alicia lifted her chin.

"Alicia." Scofield's tone was commanding. It was the voice he used when he held court and froze the villagers in their tracks. "The cave is not safe. There's nothing for us to do here. Come with me."

The judge nudged Alicia toward the entrance.

Justin glared at Pratt and saw his eyes widen – right before he pivoted. He grabbed Pratt's arm, but he was too late. The blade had already left his hand.

His heart sank as the knife flew. Had he altered its course enough to protect them?

The judge stepped in front of Alicia, the knife lodging in his shoulder.

In moments, Justin found himself in the rushing current. Pratt grabbed his hair and held him under the water.

Justin groped for the arm restraining him but couldn't get a good hold. Instead, he put his hands on top of Pratt's and trapped them. Using his hips, Justin twisted his head and body around, taking Pratt's arm with him. He kept increasing the pressure against Pratt's arm until the man released him.

Justin came up, gasping for air, amid stones pelting Pratt.

He turned toward Alicia. She stood with an arsenal of sizeable rocks, bombarding the Frenchman. She was relentless and precise.

Pratt's face was peppered with blood and bruises as stone after stone in quick succession hit him his face and chest. Her quick thinking and good work distracted the man long enough for Justin to rise to his feet.

Pratt tried to bat away the stones, but Alicia's stinging barrage came at him in a fast frenzy, hitting their mark with precision. Justin sprang at Pratt, grabbing the man by his coat front. For a moment, he was back at the mill facing Finn with Matthew close by.

"Finish the little bastard so we can go home." Matthew's voice drove him on as the fury started to build. The fierce Highland warrior had been at rest for some time. Now, he couldn't keep him at bay. He didn't want to. He let anger grow into an uncontrollable rage. The fury built to a crescendo.

He inhaled the salt air, giving breath to the sleeping warrior and let loose his battle cry, "Salamanca!"

Pratt's face blanched. Justin lifted him into the air and heaved him toward the entrance. He wasn't done.

Pratt scrambled in the rising water, trying to stand. Justin advanced.

Pratt got to his feet and stood, silently challenging him. Justin had no argument with that. This final battle was a long time coming and they both knew how it would end. Pratt threw a quick punch. Justin swatted it aside, stepped closer, and braced for the onslaught to his mid-section. He wasn't disappointed. Each punch heightened his resolve. The water was rising with Alicia and Scofield still in the cave, and he needed to get Pratt out of the way so they could leave.

Justin's right cross stunned the man. "For Richard Lewis," he said as he pressed forward, picking Pratt up only to hit him again. "For Stephen Gordon."

Pratt tried to throw punch after punch. Justin ducked and blocked and waited for his opening. It wouldn't be much longer. The timing of Pratt's onslaught slowed, with each strike growing less effective than the last. His arms drooped, leaving his face exposed.

That's right. Keep it up.

The slower Pratt threw his punches, the stronger and faster the water rushed around them. Finally out of the cave, Justin advanced, forcing Pratt down to the beach.

Justin glanced at the incoming tide. He had to end this at once, or they would be stranded on the flooded beach at the mercy of the waves and the rocks. He stepped closer.

Hit upon hit, he jabbed at the man's jaw.

Pratt took each strike until he was dazed and bloody. Justin followed with an explosive right cross. "For Matthew Terrell," he screamed, above the sound of the waves. Pratt's head bucked backwards, sending a fine spray of blood into the air and onto Justin's coat. Then he collapsed to his knees with the water almost to his chin. Justin didn't lower his guard. He waited, ready for more.

"Captain." He stopped at Barrington's word. "We'll take him."

Peter and Simon pulled Pratt to his feet and dragged him toward the path.

Barrington helped the judge. Justin turned to help Alicia, but she was gone.

A spot of blue caught his eye. She was running toward the cave. What was she doing? Justin took off after her with several men behind him. He caught her struggling in the cave up to her waist in water.

"Leave the pendant," he shouted over the rushing water.

"James," she shouted back at him. "Hurry."

"Where is he?" He rushed to her side.

"Behind the tenth boulder, I hope."

He looked toward the boulder and hurried ahead of her. They found James, his hands and feet in manacles, struggling to keep his head above water. Alicia removed the gag.

"Get out of here," he said, his voice barely a whisper.

"Justin will get us out."

"The chain is wrapped around the rock. Keep his head above the water." Justin grabbed the chain and pulled. It didn't move. He propped his foot against the boulder and tried a second time.

"It would be easier to move the rock," Alicia said, as she struggled to hold James' head above the water. Justin stared at her. He leaned around the boulder.

"Over here," he called to the men who were removing the chest. "That can wait."

James was tiring fast. He had only a matter of minutes. Their backs against the cave wall and their feet on the boulder, the men pushed as hard as they could. Nothing.

"Again," Justin said.

They tried a second time. The boulder began to move. James looked at Justin in defeat.

"Again. This time, don't stop," Justin said.

With the backs of the men against the boulder, they strained and kept up the pressure until it shifted. "*Again*," Justin commanded.

They pushed. Finally, the boulder toppled over and smashed the lock. Free of the chain, Justin reached down and heaved James over his shoulders. They hurried out of the cave, wading through waist-high water, then climbed the path as the waves licked at their heels. Justin drove everyone up and didn't stop until they reached the top.

Mr. Perkins wrapped them in blankets as they gathered. Peter and Simon took James and went to Sommer Chase. Judge Scofield was with the Land Guard commander.

Justin drew Alicia close.

"Once again, you're too late," Pratt said as he stood between the guards. "Scofield didn't fool me. The gold was a ruse. The real prize is the documents obtained and reviewed in Edinburgh. Your English troop positions are on their way to France. Your men are doomed by your own people's greed." Pratt looked down his nose and curled his lip in triumph.

"Qui vivra verra," Justin said.

"Wait and see?" Alicia asked, her brows drawn together.

The Land Guard detail was the last up from the beach. They carried the crate past Justin. Alicia stopped them.

"If it were evading the blockade for French brandy and nothing else, perhaps." Alicia tore the flag from the crate and threw out the splintered wood. "We don't bargain with our countrymen's lives. You're a fool to think otherwise. We never intended for the gold to leave England. It was all a ruse to bring. You. To. Your. Knees."

Pratt stared at the rocks in the crate.

"The English military positions?" Justin burst out laughing. "All you have are pages 16-25 from my last book. You and France have nothing for your effort. While Sommer-by-the-Sea has some fine brandy. And England? England has its gold… and you."

"You have been a worthy opponent," Pratt said. The guard moved him toward the castle, but he hesitated and called over his shoulder, "What will you do now for a villain? I am your muse."

"You're no muse, just an unimportant tool in a story to demonstrate the competency, morality, and compassion of a champion. Read the next book and you will find out how you end." Justin waited a few heartbeats to let Pratt absorb his meaning and chuckled as Pratt's smug expression faded.

"What, nothing to say?" Justin paused. "I thought not." With great satisfaction, he turned his back on the man. With the threat over, his debt to his men settled, and his blood cooled, the Highland warrior was appeased.

Barrington gestured to the guardsmen. They marched their prisoner to the castle dungeon.

"Well done, Lady Alicia. But this is no weather for an ocean swim." Barrington threw his arm around Justin. "Take my carriage and bring our heroine home. I'm sure her family is worried."

Neither of them argued. Relieved and elated, Justin helped her into the carriage.

"I worried for your safety. I didn't know what to believe when I realized you knew Commander Terrell, I mean, Pratt," Alicia said as she settled close to him.

"Pratt has been my phantom for years. An adversary that became bigger than life."

"He was correct. You fashioned your villain after him." She yawned and put her head on his shoulder.

"To me, he represented all that is evil." With a gentle touch, he turned her face and examined the bruise.

She put her hand on his. "I'm fine."

"He will pay—"

"You make it sound as if he has to pay for more than striking me. I got my revenge. I took pleasure in heaving stones at him." She pulled the blanket around her tighter.

"Yes, each one hit him precisely where you aimed. I thank you for that. Your distraction came at just the right time."

"I never miss. You can ask Effie."

He gazed at her face, settling on her mouth. *Kiss her.*

"Are you cold?"

She nodded.

"I'll keep you warm." He gathered her in his arms and held her snugly. "And safe."

"I have never felt so vulnerable, but I refused to give him that knowledge." Alicia buried her face against his throat and took a deep breath.

"You're brave and the essence of a heroine."

He lifted her chin and looked into her eyes. They would be at Hartmore Manor at any moment. The fact that he was even alone with her was scandalous. But she didn't move.

He held her attention with his eyes. She peered into them, looking for answers to questions she dared not ask. Slowly he lowered his lips to hers.

A wild tremble rolled through Alicia with the force more powerful than a great storm. Her hand came round and stroked his face, and she was rewarded with that smile, the one that drove her heart to turn over in response.

He cupped her head, his face close enough for her to see the flecks of silver in his gray eyes.

Her heart seemed to bang against her chest as he dipped his head and nuzzled her neck. She basked in the heady sensation of his warm breath against her skin and hoped for more.

His lips parted ever so slightly. Her eyes fluttered closed as she waited, hoped this kiss would feel and taste as good as their first.

He hesitated, his lips barely a breath away.

Nervous and afraid he would abandon his mission, the tip of her tongue moistened her mouth.

"You are my undoing." His kiss was slow and sent the pit of her stomach into a swirl. This was so much more than their stolen kiss in the cave.

His lips were soft, like velvet. His tongue sent shivers racing through her.

"Are you cold?" he asked as he pulled away.

She pulled him back.

"Not at all." She kissed him and found his lips still warm and moist.

His deep groan made her breathless. He deepened the kiss and her body heated until she thought she would burn up. *Oh, please. Don't ever stop.*

He pulled away and held her close.

"Kiss me again," she said.

"Nothing would please me more, but I don't want stolen kisses." He stared at her a moment, trying to make a decision. Then he kissed her sweetly on the lips.

They rode the rest of the way holding each other until the coach came to a halt at Hartmore Manor.

Justin stepped down from the carriage, lifted her out, and headed for the door.

Mr. Dodd threw open the door as he reached it. A shocked expression was on the butler's face.

"Good day, Mr. Dodd," Alicia said, as Justin – still carrying her – whisked her into the foyer.

"Alicia, is that you?" her mother called as she and the rest of the family hurried out of the drawing room.

"Mama, Papa. You're here."

"Bring her inside," her father said to Justin.

"Are you hurt?" her mother asked, hovering over her.

Beatrice and her mother fussed about her, but she wouldn't let go of Justin. He stood in the middle of the room holding her in his arms.

"Who is this man?" her father asked.

"You can put her down now," Elkington said, smiling broadly.

"Lord Hartley." Justin turned and faced her father. "I'm Captain Justin Caulfield."

"You have our thanks for bringing our Alicia home. We've all been worried about her. From the looks of her, we have had good cause."

"Before you say anything, dear," Lady Hartley said, "I must get Alicia out of these wet clothes."

"You owe me a boon," Justin said, still holding her.

"I haven't forgotten." Alicia looked at him and tried not to smile.

Justin faced Lord Hartley. "I would like the pleasure of calling on Lady Alicia."

"I have a feeling if I say 'no,' you will simply walk away with her in your arms." Her father didn't scowl. He was quite pleased with himself. "What say you, Alicia?" he asked.

She didn't take her eyes off Justin. "I would very much like for Captain Caulfield to call on me. But Justin, you needn't use your boon. I say 'yes' freely."

"Come, Alicia. You need to take off those clothes. Mrs. Dodd," her mother called over her shoulder, "bring me a poultice for this bruise."

"How did that happen?" Beatrice asked, examining it.

Justin set her on her feet, but she didn't move away from him.

"Here, have some of Elkington's brandy," her father handed Justin a half-full snifter. "You've earned it, from what he's told me."

"You'll be here when I return?" She didn't try to hide her concern.

"I must speak with Barrington. I shouldn't be long." He pulled her reticule out from his waist band and handed it to her.

"You found it." She held it to her chest then scandalously kissed his cheek. She left the room, her mother chattering away.

"The information from Lawson was essential, and your idea to swap the military positions they wanted with the pages from your book was brilliant," Elkington said.

"Lawson tried to keep his real reason secret. He told me he had a bet with our cousin Gillie and needed my help. He had promised the false troop positions to Barrington's brother all along."

"He tried to protect you," Elkington said.

"When Lawson confessed his plan, it was too late to craft something original. I did what was needed." Justin savored the fine brandy and finally relaxed.

"Alicia was brave. Fearless. You should have seen Pratt's face when she opened the crate, and it was filled with rocks, not gold."

"No gold? That's odd. Do you have any idea what she did with it?" Elkington asked. "The crate was filled with twenty pouches of gold coins worth a king's ransom. I know. I confirmed the gold was the Walmer gold for the judge."

"Alicia was aware the crate was empty. With the cave filling with the incoming tide, she must have managed to switch the gold for rocks. I suspect we will have to wait until low tide to find out."

Justin put his empty snifter on the table and faced Lord Hartley.

"Thank you for the brandy. I wish we could have met under more social circumstances."

Elkington, his arm around Justin, walked him to the door.

"You have my blessing with Alicia," Elkington said. "Not that you need it. The two of you are well-suited."

Justin walked down the path to the waiting carriage.

From her bedroom window, Alicia watched him leave the house. Before he got into the carriage, he turned and glanced at her. He didn't say anything. He didn't have to. He knew in his heart, he loved her as she loved him.

CHAPTER NINETEEN

Later that afternoon

"WE SHOULD HAVE called the doctor and had him examine Alicia."

Justin stood by the fireplace, in agreement with Lady Hartley. The poor woman was distraught, punishing the piece of linen in her hand. She sat down and got up several times.

"We applied ice to her face. The swelling has gone down and there's no fever." Lady Hartley wiped her eyes. "But she was so cold and wet. I'm worried."

Beatrice entered the drawing room. Elkington and Hartley stood. All eyes were focused on her. "Before you ask, Mama, she is quite fine and will be here straight away. She asked that we not discuss anything until she joins us." She took a seat next to her husband.

"Alicia always did want to be in the thick of things," her father said with a chuckle, as he returned to his chair.

"Perhaps we should cancel our Harvest Party. I don't know if any of us are up to it tonight," Lady Hartley said.

"Don't you dare. We have all been planning for days. Besides, Beatrice has been busy making her bilberry apple tart," Alicia said as she entered the room. She wore an ivory dress that flowed as she walked, and a long, Pomona green shawl was wrapped around her shoulders. But Justin concentrated on her face, and was relieved when he hardly made out the redness and swelling.

"Elkington, I've been trying to put all the pieces of this puzzle together." Alicia took a seat on the settee, an empty space next to her.

"What pieces, exactly?" Elkington poured more brandy.

"In speaking to Mr. Perkins, I asked about purchasing you good French brandy. I was caught off guard when he mentioned he had delivered bottles to you."

"Ah. You thought I had ill-gotten spirits." Elkington stood by the sideboard with his brandy glass raised. Beatrice spun and faced her husband. Her eyes, full of unspoken questions, didn't leave him as he moved closer to her. He put a reassuring hand on her shoulder.

"Barrington approached me with a problem Judge Scofield brought to him. A group of smugglers and spies were looking to establish themselves in Sommer-by-the-Sea. They spoke to enough people in the village to be concerned. The judge didn't want to put off the scoundrels by having the Land Guard take up residence. He asked Barrington and The League for assistance. When the leader began circulating that he had gold and needed information, Barrington became suspicious. It was right after the Walmer gold was stolen. Scofield came up with a plan to stop them forever."

Alicia glanced from Elkington to Justin, unable to say a word.

"Barrington contacted me," Justin said. "My cousin Alasdair Lawson had news and information about the Frenchman I was pursuing. They had an idea that he was involved. Anyone visiting Lawson from Sommer-by-the-Sea could warn them off. I had plans to visit with him, so I volunteered to gather the information.

"The judge and the Land Guard had a plan to stop the smugglers, but they needed to stop the person organizing the spying. No one knew who the culprit was. The details they provided gave me a good idea. I was eager to assist them. I had a score to settle."

"I had no idea," Beatrice said to her husband, "that you were in such danger."

"Not telling you was the most difficult piece of this," Elkington said, taking her hand.

"I had no idea Pratt was the Frenchman." Justin looked at Alicia. "He never revealed his face. But I witnessed enough of his abuse."

"And you both let Alicia get in the middle of this?" Beatrice stood and moved away from Elkington.

"I never imagined she would be in any jeopardy," Elkington said. "I assumed she would write one of her—"

"Little stories," Alicia completed his sentence.

Sheepishly, Elkington nodded and drank the rest of his brandy. "I wouldn't put you in any danger. Never."

"I don't think you would. The incident was educational." Alicia stood, walked over to Justin, and relieved him of his brandy. Looking into his eyes, she took a sip. His right eyebrow rose a fraction. That, along with his devilish smile, made her heart race. She returned the snifter to him.

"For both of us," he said, and finished the brandy. "This campaign and seeing you in danger opened my eyes in many ways."

"For my part, I was responsible for communication with Bamburgh Castle keeping Barrington's brother and the House of Lords apprised of the situation," Elkington told his father-in-law.

Alicia took Justin to the settee.

"I found James' League coin in your reticule. How did you come by it?" he asked.

"I found the coin by the crate. The light was too dim to make out its markings," she said.

"I assumed you found his coin and knew he was there. If you didn't know the coin was his, what made you think James was in the cave?"

"I heard a chain rattle several times, but thought the noise was from the old chains in the cave. They rattle with the wind and current.

"When Scofield and Terrell first entered the cave, Terrell said he didn't know the way, yet he corrected the judge when he took a wrong turn *and* knew where to find the chest. The final clue was when Scofield asked about James. He was supposed to be guarding the chest. It came to me when you were fighting on the beach, but Scofield wouldn't let me go back to the cave."

Justin took the opportunity to speak to Alicia while Elkington told how he helped Barrington with the Walmer gold.

"You should pursue your dream," Justin said.

Alicia turned to him. "I beg your pardon?"

"The letter you received from William Lane. Your decision is too important to be determined by a bet. That doesn't mean I, or my uncle, want you to leave Caulfield Publishing. Quite the opposite. I have read your contract and while you're obligated for one more book, we can discuss ending the contract now. The choice is up to you."

Alicia didn't say anything for several heartbeats. "You're generous with your options, but to me, my word is my bond. I will follow my contract through to the end. Afterwards, I will decide what to do."

He took her hand and gazed into her eyes.

"There is one more thing. William Lane offered to publish my stories. I understand how tempting and meaningful it is to have a premier publisher seek out your work. Rejecting his proposal even though I am taking over Caulfield Publishing was not an easy one. I did decline the offer. To my regret, not soon enough."

"That simply proves our writing is worthy no matter who our publisher is. I have no intention of letting you cry off. Perhaps an adjustment to the terms is needed."

Justin gave her a mischievous glance. "You have my attention."

"I read *In My Brother's Shadow*. It was dynamic and vivid. There was a comment in a recent review, a statement that your heroes and my heroines were excellently crafted. We capture the different essences that drive the characters, which gives them and our stories life. I found I could not forget Captain Jonathan Calum Mallory, although you have his name incorrect. The character sounded more like Captain Justin Caulfield Melrose."

He didn't move, but a fine blush ran up his throat.

Alicia turned in her chair to face him squarely. "It takes great courage to put those experiences and difficulties on paper for everyone to read. You made me experience your elation and pain. I came away understanding Captain Mallory and Mr. Melrose better. I'm proud of both and fortunate to be sitting with the one that is flesh and blood. I propose we write together, co-author a story. You write the hero and I the heroine."

Alicia waited for his response.

"My uncle told me I could learn from you. I read *The Lost Dowry*. Your characters are deep, loyal, and determined. You were the spirit of your Clarissa, today. Like you, your heroine is intelligent, a worthy companion for any man willing to accept a strong partner."

"William Lane Publishing will have nothing like our story," she said.

"We will be equal partners. That is the only way I will agree to the project," he said.

"I wouldn't have it any other way, either."

CHAPTER TWENTY

London
May 1815

ALICIA CLIMBED THE stairs of 32 Fleet Street and met Justin and his uncle in the corridor outside Caulfield Publishing.

For six months she and Justin worked on their story. Caulfield Publishing had released *The Smuggler's Cave* earlier that week.

There was nothing else for them to do. No reason to continue their daily meetings. She nearly cried herself to sleep the previous night at the thought that their time together was over.

Their creative work was outstanding, and they had grown close. They could almost finish each other's sentences. Their eagerness to be with each other hadn't waned. Last night, amidst her tears, she came to a conclusion. Determined to continue their closeness, her mission today was to propose they co-author another book.

"Alicia," Justin extended his hand as she reached the top of the stairs.

She hurried toward him and stood with him and his uncle to admire the new bronze plaque.

Justin Melrose Caulfield, Publisher.

She took out a square of linen, polished the name plate, and admired her work.

"It looks grand." She squeezed Justin's hand.

"One more task before I leave." Isaac ushered them inside.

She entered a now-orderly office. The books were organized on the shelves. Cabinets against the wall stored the stacks of papers that were once strewn over Isaac's desk. The second desk was cleared and arranged facing the other, with visitors' chairs in front of them. New dark green damask drapes hung at the windows offset with clean, crisp white sheer curtains. Everything was coordinated with the new green carpet.

Alicia removed her hat and placed it on the rack next to Justin's hat.

"Barrington sent word about Pratt's trial. Judge Scofield and Mr. Perkins testified against him. The militia was to bring him to prison."

"Was?" Her heart ached for Justin. She wondered if the memories would ever fade.

"Pratt was killed trying to escape," Justin said in an unemotional voice.

Alicia gasped.

"I can't say that I'm sorry, except for the fact that he will die only once. I died each time I lost a soldier, a friend. I've sent messages to the families of those he killed and informed them the murderer is dead by the hand of a British soldier. I hope that gives them some peace." He looked at her. The color drained from her face. "What is it?"

"Justin, it's just as we wrote. You told him his end would be in this book."

"How his life ended was inevitable, as was his attempted escape. His death lets me go forward and leave all the anguish and pain behind. I haven't felt this free and content since I was a boy." He squeezed her hand.

"I'm glad *that* is over," Isaac said. "Have you seen the *London Gazette*? The literary section?"

Isaac handed Justin the newspaper. Alicia looked over his shoulder.

"It's a review of *The Smuggler's Cave*."

"Ladies and gentlemen, I have no words to describe the literary work J. C. Melrose and Lady Alicia Hartley have crafted. J. C. Melrose doesn't allude to any imaginary horrors that he has Captain Jonathan Callum Mallory face. No, dear reader, Captain Mallory discloses the details of a gruesome war along with his terrified feelings. This story is well balanced and tempered with Lady Alicia Hartley's strong heroine Olivia Fitzwilliam who is tested by the situation as well as the hero and proves her worth.

"This reviewer had concerns about this story. Would this be two stories under one cover? I tell you, no. The authorial merits of Lady Hartley and J. C. Melrose include creating a seamless story that is compelling, spine tingling, and has you cheering for the hero and heroine all the way to their happily ever after. I will say nothing else but Outstanding!

Justin lowered the paper.

"The story is a success," Alicia whispered.

"Why are you both so surprised? I told you, writing together, you both would succeed."

Justin pulled her into his arms and spun her around.

"Put me down." Joy bubbled in her laugh and shone in her eyes.

A soft tap sounded on the door before it opened. Justin froze with Alicia in his arms. They both turned as a well-dressed man about the same age as Isaac entered.

"Isaac, are you ready?"

Justin set Alicia on her feet. He glanced at his uncle.

"William. I'm almost done here." He removed the key from his pocket and handed it to Justin. "This is the key to the office. It is yours now. Write more books with Alicia. It's time to start a new series. In this one you brought your arch-enemy to justice. You have outgrown this plot and are a better man for it."

Justin and Alicia hadn't taken their eyes off of the man that entered. "You know William Lane?" Justin asked.

"Of course I do. We have been close friends for many years," his uncle said, as he took his hat from the rack.

Alicia looked puzzled. She glanced from Justin's uncle to Lane and back again. "Did I hear you correctly?" she asked.

"You never mentioned that you were close friends," he said to his uncle. "The two of you in the same business, competitors as it is."

"I have many friends you know nothing about. Why do you find that so strange?"

Justin turned to Alicia. "Mr. Lane is a close friend of Uncle Isaac's, yet he tried to recruit us for his publishing house." He scrutinized the two men. Something was amiss. He could feel it in his bones.

"Isaac, come along. They'll be fine without you." Lane's smug smile irritated Justin.

His uncle stood next to his friend.

"What have you two done?" Justin asked.

"*Done?*" Lane asked.

"No, William. I'm tired of the charade. I told you they were clever and would find us out." Isaac stood squarely in front of Justin. "What should I tell you?"

"Everything," Justin said.

Isaac ran his hand around the rim of his hat. "All of it?" he muttered.

"Go on, you wanted to tell him," Lane said.

"William is my copy editor."

"And Isaac is mine," Lane said. "I read both your books and said the same thing that review voiced. I discussed it with Isaac. We came to the conclusion neither of you would be open to our suggestion. We couldn't believe our luck when your friend Lady Euphemia conjured up the challenge."

"It was obvious to me and William that you needed each other. I mean to say, your characters needed each other. We provided you with the opportunity." Uncle Isaac put on his hat.

"What about the offers to write for Lane Publishing? Were they part of your scheme?" Alicia asked, her tone even, but her speech clipped.

"No," William said. "I sincerely wanted to publish your books."

"You were aware I had gotten a letter from Lane Publishing," Justin said to his uncle. "And that speech, *'I leave Caulfield Publishing in your capable hands.'*" Justin swung around and stared out the window.

"Was the review in the *London Gazette* six months ago also a lie?" Alicia asked.

The two men said nothing.

"Of course it was," Justin said.

"I should have known. 'Little stories.' The signs were all there." Alicia sounded more exasperated with herself than with anyone else.

"Isaac and I wrote the review and sent it to the *London Gazette* anonymously."

Their sheepish expressions would have been laughable if she and Justin weren't angry.

He grabbed the *Gazette* from his desk. "Was this part of your scheme?" He shook the paper at them.

"Not at all. We both knew your story was excellent. Read who reviewed your book."

Alicia took the paper from Justin. She went right to the bottom of the review. "Herbert." She put the paper down. "The editor for the paper."

"I told you the story was wonderful. I wasn't wrong," Isaac said. "You both are good writers, very good writers. But together? You have a unique quality that I haven't seen before. William and I both realized your potential and were determined not to let it go to waste. Am I sorry I deceived you? Yes. Would I do it again? Definitely. Because look what you produced. If you don't believe me or William, read the reviews in the other papers and judge for yourself."

"When you didn't contact me right away about my offer, you confirmed my thinking. You both have a sense of loyalty that I admire. Success is important to you, but neither of you were willing to pay the price," Lane said.

"Another test?" Justin kept his anger in check. He wanted to throttle both men.

"Not for me, for you. I was aware of what you would do, no matter how hard I pushed you." Lane stepped closer to them. "Because I read your stories, every one of them. Your main characters are cut from the same cloth as you are. The protagonists of your stories had to be up to the challenge, just like you both were with your spy in Sommer-by-the-Sea."

"You should have found other ways to make your point. Without deception." Alicia glared at both older men, holding her more inflammatory words behind her teeth.

"For us." Justin raked his hand through his hair. "This is not a way to run a business. You don't manipulate people."

"You do what you have to do in business," his uncle said. "There are certain ways things are done. Accept them and you will be successful."

"As the new head of this publishing company, I tell you I will do what is best for the company and my authors. And I will start right now." Justin faced Alicia. "Do you agree that changes are needed?"

"I do. What did you have in mind?"

"Caulfield Publishing has been languishing, allowing William Lane to lead the market. I plan to build this company and compete against William Lane, attract progressive authors who are not afraid of writing stories pertinent to people's lives today and not just some dreams that will never come true. I also believe that this new industrial world is full of doubt and fear for many people. They need uplifting stories."

"Your happy 'little stories?'" Lane asked, a sarcastic smirk on his lips.

"Yes. Stories about people facing difficulties, hardships, all with happy endings." Alicia scowled at the man.

The eagerness Justin saw in Alicia's eyes drove him on. "I can't do this alone. If we can produce such good work writing together, imagine what we can do with this company if we're partners," Justin said.

"Partners?" she asked.

"Equal partners. We can do anything together. Say yes." He hadn't planned to ask her, but it sounded so right.

Alicia stared into his eyes. "Are you sure?"

"I have never been more certain of anything."

"Yes." She removed her glove and for a brief moment thought to spit in her hand. Knowing she'd scandalize the two older men, she simply extended it to Justin.

He accepted her hand and didn't try to hide his broad smile. For the last several weeks he dragged out the production of their book, not wanting their collaboration to end. Working with her had been delightful. They plotted and replotted. They wrote and rewrote. They were excited over each other's words, and when they had differences, they discussed them and challenged one another to think more deeply. In the end, the work benefited. He wanted more. It was more than writing. He thrived in her company.

He had never been happier.

"I'll have the papers drawn up and your name added."

He had another question for her. There were more times than he cared to recall when he had to take a risk, expose himself. He was prepared for those moments.

Why was he hesitating now? He had wanted to ask her for weeks but convinced himself to wait until after the book was done.

Then he waited until after it was published.

Now, he had run out of excuses.

"Plotting, planning, and discussing our stories is not enough. These last months, writing and working with you has been…I don't want them to stop." He took Alicia in his arms. "I want to plot, plan, and discuss our lives together. Marry me, Alicia."

"Yes. I thought you would never ask." She threw her arms around him.

Justin and Alicia glanced at the door as William and Isaac closed it behind them.

"My heart is yours, forever and always," he said.

"As mine is yours," she answered.

"You owe me a boon," he said.

"This may be the only time you hear me say this. Your wish is my command." Her smile was radiant.

He wrapped her in his arms to demonstrate just how much he loved her, and claimed his prize.

The End

About the Author

There was never a time when *USA Today* Bestseller, RUTH A. CASIE hasn't had a story in her head. When she was little, she and her older sister would dress up and act out the ones Ruth creative. Today, Ruth writes exciting and beautifully told legendary historical romances that are both rich and engaging. Her stories feature strong women and the men who deserve them, endearing flaws and all. Her stories are full of, 'edge of your seat' suspense, mind-boggling drama, and a forever-after romance.

She lives in New Jersey with her hero, three empty bedrooms and a growing number of incomplete counted cross-stitch projects. Before she found her voice, she was a speech therapist (pun intended), client liaison for a corrugated manufacturer, and vice president at an international bank where she was a product/ marketing manager, but her favorite job is the one she's doing now—writing romance. Ruth hopes her stories become your favorite adventure.

Fun facts about Ruth:

1. She filled her passport up in one year.
2. She has three series. The Druid Knight is a time travel romance. The Stelton Legacy is a historical fantasy about the seven sons of a seventh son. Havenport Romances are contemporary romantic suspense stories. She also writes for the Pirates of Britannia connected world.

3. She did a rap with her son to "How Many Trucks Can a Tow Truck Tow If a Tow Truck Could Tow Trucks."

4. When she cooks she dances around the kitchen.

5. Her sudoku books is in the bathroom and that's all she'll say about that!

Social Media Links:

Website:
ruthacasie.com

Instagram:
instagram.com/ruthacasie

Facebook private reader's page, Casie Café:
facebook.com/groups/963711677128537

Facebook Author Page:
facebook.com/RuthACasie

Twitter:
twitter.com/RuthACasie

BookBub:
bookbub.com/authors/ruth-a-casie

Amazon:
amazon.com/author/ruthacasie

Goodreads:
goodreads.com/author/show/4792909.Ruth_A_Casie

YouTube:
bit.ly/3hI5eQr

www.ingramcontent.com/pod-product-compliance
Lightning Source LLC
Chambersburg PA
CBHW070943190726
48292CB00004B/1315